CRIMSON STORM

CRIMSON STORM

A DYSTOPIAN VAMPIRE FANTASY ROMANCE

AMY PATRICK

Oxford South Press

CONTENTS

ABOUT
CRIMSON STORM

Abigail Byler is a resolute pacifist. And a vampire.

Believing she can never be with the guy she loves and knowing she doesn't fit in at the Crimson Court, Abbi has left the hills and caverns of Virginia for California and the Human-Vampire Coalition where she hopes to make the best of the unexpected turn her life has taken.

That's easier said than done when her heart still longs for her first love, Reece—and when tensions between humans and vampires in America are rapidly increasing.

The last thing Abbi intends to do is return to the Bastion—it's too dangerous for her there—in every way. But when her life takes another shocking twist, she may have no other choice than to make the perilous cross-country journey and face the vampire who turned her—and the one she still loves.

This time, though, she won't be alone. And the vampire queen of the Crimson Court is not going to like it when she finds out who's coming to dinner.

Sign up now for Amy Patrick's VIP List and get a free book, exclusive content, and other fun freebies, plus book and sale news!
Join the VIP list here: https://bit.ly/APsVIPs

Keep in touch with Amy Patrick!
Join Amy Patrick's Peeps on Facebook
Like Amy on Facebook
Hang with Amy on Goodreads
Follow Amy on Bookbub
Follow Amy on Instagram

The Crimson Accord Series
Crimson Born
Crimson Storm
Crimson Bond
Crimson Crown

The Hidden Saga
Hidden Deep (FREE download)
Hidden Heart
Hidden Hope
The Sway (FREE when you join my list!)
Hidden Darkness (Dark Court, 1)
Hidden Danger (Dark Court, 2)
Hidden Desire (Dark Court, 3)

ix

1

REECE

My brothers and I darted from the shadow of one historic building to the next in Charlottesville's deserted open-air downtown mall, tracking the rogue vampire.

She'd hit the University of Virginia campus hard, slaughtering four students in one dorm before escaping into the night.

We weren't sure if she was a student herself. All we knew was what we'd heard on the police scanner—a young white female had been seen running from the dorm, covered in blood, and judging from the victims' wounds, they suspected the perpetrator had been a vampire.

Not good.

My fellow Bloodbound soldiers and I loaded up into a dark, nondescript van and speeded for the city that was far too close to the Bastion for comfort. We needed to neutralize the rogue quickly before she could call any more attention to herself—or to us.

Her trail had been easy to follow. She was a newbie for sure and had most likely *not* been educated at the Bastion. If she had been, she'd know how to feed on humans without killing them, or at least without making such a public mess of it.

My guess was that she *was* a student and had been attempting to feed on animals instead of drinking human blood after being turned. That was a sure path to crazy-town and incidents like this one.

I should know.

"There. Just to your north," I whispered into my comm, alerting Kannon, who was closest to the rogue's location. "She'll come out of the alley in about two seconds."

"Affirmative," my friend said. "This sorority girl has just been to her last human kegger."

Sure enough, the hint of movement I'd spotted in the dark alley was our target. The instant she stepped from between the buildings onto the main brick-lined thorough-fare of the pedestrian shopping area, Kannon tackled her and strapped her arms.

"Whoa, she's got some kick to her," I heard him say into his comm as I jogged toward his location with two other Bloodbound flanking me. "She must have really gorged herself on blood."

We arrived just as Kannon flipped the girl over. Her eyes were wild, her blood-stained teeth gnashing as she struggled against the restraints.

My guess about her identity had been correct based on her attire—a dirty frat party t-shirt and a pair of tiny athletic shorts. She wore a pair of small diamond studs in her ears. Her feet were bare. The toenails were painted, as were her fingernails, so her animal-blood-induced delirium was probably a recent development.

"Hold still," Kannon ordered, attempting to strap her ankles.

Kneeling, I held her legs so he could complete the job. "We're not going to hurt you. We'll get you some help. Don't be afraid."

Unable to kick now and most likely unable to understand me, the rogue bucked her body and screamed. She followed that up with a powerful head butt to my ribcage.

I glanced back over my shoulder to the pair of Bloodbound standing behind me—staring at their *phones*. "A little help here guys? I mean, I heal fast, but cracked ribs still hurt like hell."

"Sorry," said Michael, the younger of the two. "I was checking my feeds. Reception at the Bastion sucks."

He squatted and pressed down on the girl's shoulders while the other soldier, Rick, sneered. "Why do you waste your time on that garbage? I was checking my stock portfolio."

He drew a roll of black duct tape from his pack and placed a strip over the rogue's mouth so she couldn't use her teeth as weapons against us. Her bite wouldn't kill us, but it would leave evidence of vampire blood here in the mall, and I really didn't feel like spending the rest of the evening scrubbing the brick walkway.

Completely immobilized now, the female vampire finally gave up the struggle. Kannon let out a loud breath then looked over at me and laughed.

"Well, that was easy."

My laughter joined his. "Please tell me I wasn't this bad."

"Worse," he responded with a good-natured grin.

Kannon and his team had hunted me down and captured me in an operation much like this one—only I'd spent several weeks on the run after turning instead of a few days.

And I'd done far more damage.

The memories haunted me. How had Abbi managed to stand being around me? I was little better than a rabid animal when they'd dragged me to the Bastion and thrown me in a medical holding cell where I'd refused treatment, refused to even speak to her.

And still she'd returned each day, spending hours on end talking to me, reading to me. Her sweet voice had reached inside my muddled brain and latched onto my last remaining shred of sanity like a lifeline.

She might have been the only person on earth who could have pulled me back from that abyss. It was a good thing there had been bars between us because my body and soul had responded to her so powerfully I'd wanted to grab her and drag her off to the cavern's remotest corner where I could keep her all to myself forever.

I'd actually been a little afraid for her to be around me. But her quiet courage seemed to know no bounds. Neither did her sweetness. She was hands down the bravest, kindest, most beautiful person who ever lived, and I loved her beyond reason.

And there it was, the sweet pain that wrapped itself around my heart and squeezed like a boa constrictor anytime I let myself think of her. Which was far too often.

The torment of her absence was only slightly better than the agony of her presence. Having her close but always out of reach would have driven me mad.

I would have eventually caved to the temptation and gotten us both beheaded.

So it was good she was gone.

Really, it was.

I was just sad about the way she'd left. I knew Abbi didn't understand my decision to take the Bloodbound vows and pledge myself to Imogen for eternity.

But even if I hadn't gone through with the ceremony, even if Abbi hadn't left, I would still have lost her. Because Imogen would have told her what I did.

There was no way Abbi's love for me could survive that.

Kannon and I lifted the rogue vampire between us as our brothers kept watch. Moving toward the van parked nearby, we passed under a streetlamp, and I caught the glint of a ring on the girl's left ring finger. It was a silver band with an eternity knot design. A promise ring.

Another spasm gripped my heart. I'd given Abbie the vampire equivalent when I'd handed her that pendant necklace containing my blood. It was a stupid thing to do, but I hadn't been able to bear thinking of her out there in the world, moving on with her life and forgetting about me entirely.

She'd probably tossed it in the garbage by now—as she should. It had been over a year since she'd left the Bastion with her friends, Kelly and Heather, and gone to Los Angeles to work for Sadie Aldritch, the leader of the Vampire-Human Coalition.

She was better off there. There was certainly nothing left for her here.

Though it killed me to think of her with some other guy taking moonlight strolls along the Southern California beaches...

Stop *thinking about it*

Though it killed me to picture her with someone else, I did want her to be happy. I wanted her to be safe.

I couldn't guarantee she'd be either of those things if she was here with me. And so I would try—once again—to let go of her memory the way I'd let go of her hand that night.

Maybe one day I'd actually succeed.

2

ABIGAIL

I missed butter. The hand-churned kind Mamm used to melt and pour over kettle-cooked popcorn back when I was a kid.

Back when I was human.

Rubbing a palm over my stomach to dismiss the phantom hunger pangs, I watched the guard in his tower shove his hand into a bag of the microwave kind. Each time he brought a handful of popcorn to his mouth and chewed, the glowing tip of his specially outfitted ultraviolet assault rifle bobbed up and down.

"What are you looking at leech?" he barked when he noticed me. "Keep moving. And stop staring at me."

He probably thought he was clever for calling me a slur I'd heard at least a hundred times before.

I shook my head and strolled along the perimeter of the yard. The man acted as if I was the one with the deadly weapon in hand, as if I could mesmerize him with just a look.

Of course that was ridiculous, one of the many bits of misinformation that had been spread about my race. At least it kept the guards here at the Merced Safety Center from getting too close to us.

Unless you counted Gatlin. He liked getting a little *too* close to the female vampires being detained here—especially during daylight hours when we were nearly catatonic with sleepiness. I did my best to stay as far away from him as possible and off his radar.

At the moment, he patrolled the western perimeter of the exercise yard, walking back and forth just outside the twenty-foot-high electrified fence that separated the humans from the vampires, the wide brim of his ever-present Outback hat shading his smug face from the bright overhead security lights.

He was fond of tipping that hat in mock respect whenever he noticed one of the elder vampires looking at him.

"Top of the evening to ya," he'd say and sneer in that mean way of his, perhaps unaware that the oldest among us were often the most dangerous.

Luckily for Gatlin—and all his fellow prison guards— the vampires in this place were more likely than not pacifists, the very *last* among our kind who'd bite them or even want to.

That was how we'd ended up here—we'd come along peacefully when we'd been told our sudden arrests were "just routine" and would be "resolved quickly" and that our property and personal belongings would be restored to us "with all haste" after it was confirmed we weren't part of the violent vampire resistance movement.

All lies, sadly. I'd been here for the past month without so much as a meeting with the facility's administrators or a lawyer or judge or anyone else who might answer my questions, take my statement, or let me go home.

My situation wasn't unique. Nathaniel Bradford, an

ancient vampire who'd arrived at the Safety Center a week ago, told me he'd simply been going for a stroll outside his Beverly Hills mansion when the police slapped platinum handcuffs on his wrists and forced him into the back of a cruiser.

He'd been growing increasingly frustrated as the days passed with no resolution. Like me, he paced the perimeter fence tonight, trapped and afraid.

"Excuse me, sir," he said to Gatlin through the electrified chain link. "There has been a mistake. I've committed no crime. I demand to speak to the administrator."

The guard laughed. "Well you'd better *stop* demanding or what you'll get is one of these solar bullets in your cold, white ass," he shouted.

He needn't have yelled. Nathaniel could have heard the slightest whisper clearly. We all could.

"You can't hold me here for no reason," the elderly vampire informed him. "This is America. I'm an American citizen. I'm entitled to due process. I fought in the Revolutionary War for Heaven's sake."

The guard looked more rattled than I'd ever seen him. He took a step back. "Well then you're old enough to know better than to argue with the business end of a UV rifle."

"I doubt you even know how to handle that weapon," Nathaniel taunted. "Your hands are shaking like those of an untested youth. In fact, I've fought alongside fifteen-year-olds who quaked less. If we'd had cowards like you in our ranks, the Revolution would have failed, and you'd be speaking with a British accent, which I must say in your case would be a vast improvement."

The guard shouldered his rifle, pointing it at Nathaniel's face. "I'll *show* you how I handle my weapon, you blood-sucking parasite."

Gesturing to one side with the gun barrel, he said, "Now shut your mouth and get back to your area before I light you up—permanently."

The ancient vampire's fangs emerged from between his lips.

Oh no. This wasn't going to be good.

It wasn't a purposely threatening expression or even one of thirst. It was simply a natural vampire reflex, a reaction to the bald aggression in the other man's voice. I'd had to work hard to hide the automatic response in myself at times when I'd been taunted and insulted by the guards here.

Gatlin backstepped farther from the fence, still training his rifle on Nathaniel.

"Get back. Don't think showing me your fangers is gonna get you in to see the warden any sooner. You think you're so smart—I can't believe you haven't figured it out by now... you're never getting out of here. None of you stiffs are."

A growl rumbled in Nathaniel's throat, but his voice remained calm. "I'm afraid that answer is unacceptable."

His fangs slid fully from their sockets, their ultra-white color gleaming in the moonlight as he approached the fence, stretching his hands toward it as if to rip the steel links apart.

Maybe he could. I'd never met a vampire as old as him. I wasn't sure what they were capable of. Maybe the electric current wouldn't affect him as it did the younger members of our race.

His pale fingers contacted the metal. And nothing happened.

No blue spark, no buzz of high voltage. Nothing to keep Nathaniel from scaling the fence and jumping to freedom on the other side.

"Whoa—wait a minute. What did you do?" the guard yelled, falling back a few more steps.

"As a wise friend of mine once said, 'Give me liberty or give me death,'" Nathaniel said and began to climb, moving so quickly his body blurred in my vision.

"You want death? You got it Grampa," the guard yelled in a panicky tone. He raised his rifle and fired.

Nathaniel fell to the concrete. After a second, he clutched his stomach and began screaming. A hole appeared in his midsection, its burning edges spreading rapidly outward until the cavity expanded to erode the vampire's entire chest then his neck and abdomen.

The screaming stopped.

It was the first time I'd seen someone die here. And I'd never seen someone die like *that*.

I'd heard about what the new UV weapons could do, of course. They were discussed on the news as either the latest and greatest form of "home protection"—or the harbinger of mass genocide—depending on what network you watched. I'd never dreamed they'd be so effective though.

Seeing Nathaniel, who'd lived through twelve wars and who knew *how* many battles, reduced to a smoldering pile of disconnected limbs sickened me.

It also reminded me of something Reece had said during one of our walks together not long before I'd left the Bastion for California.

They won't rest until every last one of us is burned from the consciousness of humanity.

At the time I'd believed he was simply cynical. Now I'd begun to wonder if he'd been the smartest of us all.

3

BULLIES

"Any of the rest of you bloodsuckers want some?" Gatlin yelled in a shaky voice.

Striding close to the fence again, he pointed his rifle at the small group of vampires who'd ventured near to investigate Nathaniel's remains—or perhaps test the barrier themselves.

They scattered and retreated, leaving the guard smiling.

"That's right. The president has assured us there's plenty more of those UV rounds coming—more than enough to take care of *all* of you." He lifted a walkie-talkie to his mouth. "Get someone out here to test the western barrier. *Now*."

Behind me, the sound of whimpers was followed by a soft sob. I turned to see Kelly and Heather huddled together, staring in horror at the place where Nathaniel had stood only moments earlier.

We'd been together when we were arrested in Los Angeles and tried to keep an eye on each other at all times here in the prison camp.

While none of us were having a good time, I worried for

Heather most of all. She was growing thinner by the day, and she frequently got the shakes. She had the vampire equivalent of low blood sugar.

Before we'd been incarcerated, she'd managed it by drinking small doses of blood frequently. But here we had no control over when we were fed and how much. It was never enough—for any of us—which frankly was dangerous for our human captors.

I walked over to my friends, whispering for them to follow me to the other side of the enclosure.

"What's going to happen to us, Abbi?" Kelly asked.

"Did you hear what Gatlin said? He said none of us are getting out of here," Heather said. There were tears in her eyes, making their lilac shade appear even lighter.

"He was just talking tough," I assured her, instilling as much confidence in my voice as I could muster. "Of course we're getting out of here. It's a temporary holding facility. As Mr. Bradford said, we're American citizens. The Accord gave us full rights. We won't antagonize the guards as he did. We'll follow the rules and keep our heads down, and we'll be fine until Sadie is able to secure our release. I'm sure she's working on it as we speak."

Please God let Sadie be working on it.

In spite of my confident words and tone of voice I was growing more worried with each passing week in confinement.

Nathaniel had been foolish to challenge the armed guard, but he'd been right about one thing—it was wrong that we hadn't been allowed to speak to an administrator by now or anyone outside the facility.

"How would Sadie even know where we are?" Kelly argued. "They took all our phones."

A cold slice of fear bisected my empty belly. "I'm sure

when we didn't show up for work, she started looking for us," I said. "You know how smart she is. She'll figure out where we are and come for us—all of us. We're innocent. We won't be here much longer."

When I'd first heard about the Safety Centers, I hadn't worried too much, assuming only those who'd violated the Accord were being sent to them.

I hadn't seen much of the world before my seventeenth birthday, having grown up in an Amish community far removed from the outside "English" world. I was barely aware of the Crimson Accord until I became a vampire myself.

In my classes at the Bastion, I'd learned that prior to the signing of the Accord things had been ugly, with humans being drained or turned against their will and vampires being hunted and mostly in hiding.

But once our numbers had grown significant enough, Sadie Aldritch, the leader of the Vampire-Human Coalition, had approached John F. Kennedy, the American president at the time, and convinced him a peaceful treaty between vampires and humans was the best thing for everyone.

Kennedy had interceded with other world leaders, and for the past sixty years, humans and vampires had co-existed peacefully, except for in a very few holdout countries that still refused to acknowledge the existence of vampires.

Vampires had become active members of their communities, and though there were always a few bad apples, most were considered exemplary workers who never called in sick, required no health insurance, happily covered night shifts, and made amazing long-haul truck drivers.

Older vampires I knew told stories of how glorious it was to be able to go out in public for the first time without fear of being staked or shot. Red fireworks still lit up the night every twenty-fifth of April in celebration of Accord Day.

The past few months though, had been disturbing. Vampire neighbors of ours in Burbank, a dermatologist and an advertising executive, had disappeared without a trace. Heather had been feeding their dog in their absence.

Another friend, Larkin, had been abruptly fired from her research job and despite an Ivy League education and spotless employment record had been unable to find another one in her field. She'd had to leave the city and take a much less prestigious and lower paying job in San Francisco.

And then there was the election. Graham Parker, who'd run for president on a hardline anti-vamp platform, had quickly amassed a small but very vocal following who harbored hatred toward vampires—any and all vampires.

His campaign had worked hard to stir up fears among the rest of the humans in our country. Apparently, it had succeeded. He'd won the race.

He hadn't yet taken office, but since Election Day things had been rapidly changing.

It seemed the Accord was unraveling, and the old animosity and suspicion between vampires and humans was bubbling up again. I only hoped Sadie and her allies at the Coalition would be able to keep it from boiling over into an all-out war.

And that she could get me and my friends—and the other innocent vampires—out of this place soon.

A bell rang, and the vampires in the yard raised their heads, almost as one.

"Ration time," called Phillip. He was one of the nice guards, and most nights he was the one who delivered our nightly meal.

Lining up with my fellow detainees, I waited for him to hand me the small blood bag that would sustain me for another day. It wasn't buttered popcorn, but it got the job done.

Without it, I'd weaken and eventually desiccate like any other member of my species would without proper nutrition.

Phillip smiled at me as I reached the front of the line, the wrinkles around his kind blue eyes deepening. "Good evening, Miss Abigail. I heard we had a bit of excitement out in the yard tonight. You doing okay?"

I nodded and accepted the vinyl bag he offered. "I'm all right. Thank you Phillip."

"Listen, I'm sorry you had to see that. You be sure and stay out of Gatlin's way, okay sweetheart? He's been on edge lately and spoiling for a fight. Just stay clear of him."

"I will. Thank you," I said before moving aside for the next prisoner in line.

"Oh dear, Margaret, you're still looking peaked tonight," Phillip said. "Still having trouble sleeping?"

I looked back over my shoulder to see her shuffle forward. Margaret had arrived at the Center two days ago. A senior citizen, she was the sickliest, most confused vampire I'd ever seen.

Well, almost. When I'd first met Reece, he'd been nearly insensible from malnutrition and blood poisoning.

"I think it's that rabbit blood still in my system. I'll be okay soon. This will help," she told the kindly guard. "Thank you, sir."

Moving slowly, she went to sit on one of the small grassy patches in our enclosure. For a moment, I watched her fumble with the small stopper at the end of the rubber tubing.

I went and sat beside her, holding out my hand for the bag. "Let me see that."

She clutched the blood to her chest. "Please. No. I need it. I'm sick. I was starving before they picked me up for vagrancy. I got so desperate I started drinking rabbits and squirrels and such. I'll give you my rations tomorrow—I promise."

Blinking in shock, I dropped my hand. "No. I'm not trying to take it from you. I was going to help you open it."

"Here." I offered her my blood bag, which I'd already opened. "Take mine."

After a moment's hesitation, she dropped her own bag and snatched the open one from my hand, sucking frantically at the tube. I tried to ignore the gnawing hunger in my own stomach.

"You should be okay in a few weeks. I've seen animal poisoning before. It's reversible if you haven't been doing it too long."

She nodded and continued drinking. "Thank you. Sorry I was rude. It's just that one of the others took my rations the first night. I really was starting to think I might die in here."

"Someone took it from you?"

Maybe I shouldn't have been surprised. It was probably unreasonable to assume every vampire in here was an upstanding citizen who'd been falsely accused. I guessed sometimes my mind reverted back to my human days and the community I'd grown up in where crime was nearly non-existent and everyone shared what they had.

"Who was it?" I demanded to know.

Margaret looked around then whispered under her breath. "Over there. The big one with the long, black hair."

I followed her gaze to a huge male vampire leaning

against the wall of the barracks. He was laughing with another male I'd never met.

Both of them looked rough, scary, like the Bloodbound soldiers I'd known back at the Bastion. Like Reece.

They were the type of vampires the anti-vampers always pointed to when they tried to stir up fear. The type who gave us all bad names and made us targets.

Bullies.

Aggressive energy charged through my muscles, causing me to clench my fingers into fists and grind my teeth together. Part of me would have loved to march over there and demand restoration of Margaret's missing rations.

The smarter part of me decided to follow my own advice and not draw attention to myself. I picked up Margaret's discarded bag from the grass, opened it, and handed it back to her.

"Take this one too. It'll help you recover faster."

She stopped drinking. "No. I can't. You'll have no rations. You'll get weak."

Giving her a smile, I got to my feet. "I'm not hungry. Besides, it's not like I'm going to be running any marathons. I'll eat tomorrow night."

She clasped the second bag gratefully. "Bless you child. What is your name?"

"It's Abigail Byler. My friends call me Abbi."

"Abbi, I won't forget this. When we both get out of here, I'm going to repay your kindness," she vowed.

"Oh, that's not necessary. It's really not that big of a deal—"

My sentence was cut off by the roar of a loud motor followed by a crash of metal and the sound of screams.

4

OUT OF TIME

At first I thought it was a terrorist attack.

I'd seen news reports about incidents where radical anti-vampers had driven vehicles into crowds of vampires at popular outdoor nighttime gathering spots.

But no, that didn't make sense. For one thing, we were already incarcerated, which I assumed would make the vamp haters happy.

For another thing, the armed men who emerged from the SUV after crashing it through the western fence were motioning to a group of vampires nearby, encouraging them to get inside the vehicle.

One of the men simply stood outside of it, his arms spread out to the sides, head tipped back to the sky, no gun in sight.

"Come on," one of the other men yelled toward the inmates and waved his arms above his head. "We'll get you out of here. Don't worry about the fence. It's deactivated."

No one seemed to be taking him up on his offer. Vampires poured through the opening in the broken fence, bypassing the men and escaping the grounds of the Safety Center into the foothills that lay beyond it.

Some stuck around long enough to kill the guards stationed around the perimeter and up in the watch tower. I couldn't see Phillip. I hoped he'd made it back inside before the chaos erupted.

One escapee stopped just outside the fence where Gatlin now lay injured and bleeding. It was the large, black-haired soldier-type.

He knelt to the ground and started drinking from the man's wounds, ignoring his screams of terror.

"Help. Get him off me. Get him off," the guard screamed, though there was no one with a pulse left to hear.

Conflicting feelings battled inside me. Dismay. Satisfaction. Thirst.

The last one was self-explanatory. I hadn't taken my ration tonight, and the scent of fresh blood—Gatlin's and that of the other guards—filled the night air.

Dismay because I didn't agree with taking blood from an unwilling human, particularly a helpless, injured one.

And satisfaction because if anyone deserved to be drained, it was Gatlin. Still, I moved in their direction, intending to intervene. The death of a guard at vampire hands wouldn't bode well for the rest of our kind.

If I'd learned anything from Sadie it was that change could only come from setting a good example for other vampires and demonstrating to the humans that we weren't all soulless monsters driven by our unholy thirst.

By the time I reached them, the big male had been joined by his friend from the yard and a female vampire.

"Stop, please," I begged them. "You're going to get us all in trouble."

One of the males raised his head, his lips shining and dark with blood. "In trouble? We're in *prison*. Wake up. If you were smart, you'd join us. He deserves it. Feed on this bastard, make him pay. You can strengthen yourself and escape before the backup arrives. Either way you'd better hurry. One of the guards is bound to have made a distress call."

The woman chimed in. "At least run. Following the rules won't save you now, honey. When the backup arrives, they're going to shoot first and ask questions later, and I doubt they'll be keeping track of who's a pacifist and who's not. There's not going to be any throwing yourself on the mercy of the court. You can't trust any of the humans. Fighting back is our only chance."

"What should we do?" Kelly asked. I turned to see her approaching with Heather. Their eyes were wide and frightened, taking in the chaos all around us.

I was paralyzed by indecision. It wasn't like we were anonymous and could simply disappear and go back to our lives. The Safety Center had records of all our names and addresses.

If we escaped, they'd only track us down, and then they'd have a legitimate reason for holding us and confiscating all our property and financial assets.

But what if the female attacker was right? What if the arriving troops started firing at random? What if they'd been given orders to shoot every vampire in the camp?

"I don't know. I don't even know where to go," I told my friends. "But I don't think we can stay here."

A new voice entered the conversation. "I can help you. Come with me. I'll get you to safety."

I turned to see one of the humans from the truck jogging toward us. He was younger than the others, around my age.

He carried a handgun down by his side, but not the kind outfitted with anti-vampire ammunition.

Did that mean he was a vamp ally? Had he and his associates come to break us out?

Had Sadie sent them?

A few seconds later the answers to those questions were no longer my main concern. A group of guards dressed in riot gear burst from the doors of the Safety Center barracks, yelling for us to drop to the ground with our hands behind our heads.

They were at the far end of the yard, but we had only seconds left to decide which way to go—obey and remain prisoners, perhaps have the blame for the attack on the fence and the deaths of the other guards placed on us—or leave with the mysterious men who'd crashed their SUV through the fence.

"We've got to go," the young guy said, sounding breathless. "It's now or never. Trust me. They'll kill you if you stay."

"Abbi?" Kelly asked in an anxious whine. "What should we do?"

I still wasn't sure it was the right thing, but I said, "Let's go."

The young guy nodded and motioned for us to go ahead of him. "Run to the truck. I'll give you some cover."

As we bolted toward the vehicle, which had now circled around to face away from the Safety Center, I heard several loud pistol shots followed by the sound of UV rifles firing. A glowing round whizzed by my ear.

Beside me, a vampire I didn't know burst into flame and fell to the ground, writhing. Heather screamed, stopping in place. I grabbed the back of her bright yellow uniform, pulling her along.

"Don't stop. Run. Keep running."

We reached the SUV in seconds and dove into its open back door. One vampire in prison garb was already inside. Margaret. She was seated in the darkened third row, huddled into a corner.

Thank God she's safe.

There were two human men in the front seat and another man in the back row with Margaret. I couldn't see him well, but his heat signature told me he was human.

The driver twisted back to look at me. He was a middle-aged man with sparse gray hair and piercing dark eyes. He was very underweight for his height with a gaunt face.

"Where's Shane?" he demanded.

I spun back to look for the younger guy who'd spoken to us. "He was right behind us."

And then there he was, charging toward the SUV and leaping onto the bench seat beside me. He slammed the door behind him and made a chopping motion with his hand and forearm, breathing hard.

"Go. Go. Drive. We're outta time."

The older man threw the SUV into gear and punched the gas pedal, causing the vehicle to leap forward. Metallic pings and thumps sounded throughout the cabin, no doubt from the guards firing at us.

As we sped down the narrow access road away from the Safety Center, I shifted in my seat to peer through the vehicle's rear window, searching for headlights or any other signs of pursuit. There were none.

"Why aren't they coming after us?" I asked no one in particular.

The man in the back seat grinned and held up a box cutter. "Maybe they would if all the tires on their trucks weren't flat."

"Who are you people?" I asked.

The front seat passenger turned around to face me, giving me a little shock.

I know him.

5

A FAVOR

He was a guard at the Safety Center. Glenn, I thought his name was. I'd seen him only a few times—I assumed he usually worked the day shift while we were all sleeping.

Shane was the one who answered. "We're friends. Don't worry. We're not going to hurt you."

"Did Sadie send you?"

"Who's Sadie?" he asked.

"Sadie Aldritch, the leader of the Vampire-Human Coalition."

"Oh no." The driver groaned. "Don't tell me you're one of those."

"One of what?" Heather asked.

"Those hippie peacenik vamps. Fantastic. Dammit Glenn—how could you let this happen?" He swore again and shot a glare at the man beside him.

"Sorry. It got real crazy real fast," the front seat passenger explained. "I thought I'd never figure out how to turn off the current to that western fence. By the time I got it shut off and made it out to the yard, most of them were gone already. I'm impressed we pulled it off at all with only a few hours' planning. At least we got *some*."

I shook my head, thoroughly confused. Why would one of the guards help us escape?

And the driver should have been *thankful* we were pacifists who believed in Sadie's peaceful philosophy and leadership.

If we weren't, he and his companions might not be in possession of their full blood supply at the moment.

The prison rations had been barely adequate, keeping us alive but only at a subsistence level. I was weak, edgy, and ravenous, and I knew my fellow vampires were too.

"Wait—*what* is going on here?" Kelly asked. "Did you mean to rescue someone else?"

My mind flashed back to the large, warrior-looking types who'd stolen Margaret's rations and killed Gatlin. Maybe they *had* been a couple of Imogen's soldiers, and *she'd* orchestrated the jailbreak to get them out.

The ruler of the Crimson Court valued her Bloodbound soldiers above all else—even me. Especially me.

Maybe Glenn was a mole for her or something? It didn't seem like her style to rely on a human, but I would put nothing past her if it served her purposes.

"Just be grateful we got you out of there, okay?" the driver said in a highly irritated tone. "You'd probably be a little puff of smoke by now if we hadn't."

"What does that mean?" I looked at Shane because he seemed to be the friendliest of our liberators.

"I guess they don't let you guys watch the news in those places, huh? It's Inauguration Day. One of the first things President Parker did when he left the podium after taking the oath of office was sign an executive order regarding the Safety Centers and the vamps in prison," he said.

An invisible hand grabbed my throat, making it difficult to speak. "What order?"

"To uh... liquidate their population. Tomorrow morning." Shane's face crinkled in an almost embarrassed expression.

"Liquidate? What does that mean?" Heather asked.

I knew what the word meant, and it wasn't good. "They're going to *kill* all the people in all the Safety Centers?"

"Not the people," Glenn the guard piped up from the front passenger seat, shooting a cocky grin over his left shoulder. "Just the vamps."

"Hey, they're people too," Shane said, but Glenn just chuckled and turned to face the front windshield again.

"No offense," the guard said in a tone that was far from apologetic. "A little gratitude might be nice, by the way."

"Thank you," I bit out.

The driver smiled at me in the rearview mirror. "That's better. Now how bout all of you shut up and let me focus on driving? The sun's gonna be coming up in a couple hours, and if we don't make it home before that, all our heroics are gonna be for nothin'. This SUV isn't treated for daytime vamp driving."

Interesting. It must really have been a quickly planned operation for them to have arrived so close to dawn.

Or... maybe they'd planned it that way so we'd have very little time left to find shelter if we decided *not* to go along with them.

I turned to Shane, speaking quietly. "Where are you taking us?"

"To my uncle's house." He pointed to the driver. "That's my Uncle Terry."

Gesturing to the guard in the passenger seat, he said,

"That's my Uncle Glenn. They're brothers. You and your friends can spend the day at the house and leave when the sun goes down tomorrow night. Don't worry. Like I said, no one's going to hurt you. Terry just wants a favor."

Ah. Now it was starting to make sense. The men didn't strike me as pro-vampire activists or do-gooders of any kind.

"What kind of favor?" I asked, but Glenn shot me a warning look.

"Quiet now. We'll tell you when we get there."

Okay then.

I wasn't sure what favor our "liberators" were after, but I *was* grateful. If there was something *legal* I could do to help the man, I would.

Now if he wanted me and my friends to use our speed and strength to rob a convenience store or something, he was out of luck. With President Parker officially in office, it was possible vampires caught committing crimes could be shot on sight with no repercussions.

Maybe Imogen was right.

She had warned that we couldn't trust the humans to honor the Accord, that eventually they'd turn on us. That was why she offered sanctuary to any vampires who wanted it and had formed her own personal army, the Bloodbound.

No. I refused to believe it. I had to trust that Sadie would be able to reason with the new president and make him see the Crimson Accord was still a benefit to society. It terrified me to think of what would happen if it were to be dissolved.

Peace between vampires and humans was the *only* answer. I'd believed in that enough to leave home over it, enough to dedicate my life to working for Sadie and her cause.

Enough to leave Reece behind.

6

YOU OWE ME

The last few miles of the drive were a harrowing race with extinction.

Shane's Uncle Terry cursed under his breath and sweated profusely, flooring the accelerator and taking curves at terrifying speed. I prayed we wouldn't tip over and be forced out into the quickly approaching daylight—and that the police didn't notice his erratic driving and pull us over.

As the sky lightened, I could see the man's face in the mirror more clearly. The gray tint of his skin.

He was ill. A sense of unease tightened my muscles as a suspicion developed about the "favor" he planned to ask.

Not that. Please not that.

We pulled into the garage of a nice suburban home in Davis just before the sun crested the horizon. When the garage door lowered, we all climbed out of the SUV, and Terry invited us into the house.

Once inside, we stood in the kitchen together, looking around in awkward silence. It was one of those open concept homes where you could see the living area from the kitchen. There was light wood furniture and a large TV set over the fireplace.

Though there were some feminine touches like throw pillows on the sofa and a pair of matching lamps on the side tables flanking it, everything looked slightly dated, as if perhaps the woman of the house hadn't lived there in some time.

I'd noted some major differences between human homes and vampire homes. For instance, windows that weren't covered by drapes or blinds.

Also, kitchens in vampire homes were typically spotless, unused as they were for food preparation.

This kitchen smelled like fish. I could tell from my friends' reactions they noticed it too and weren't any more thrilled at the offensive odor than I was.

They were also exhausted, as was I. It had been a long night, and even on a regular day, most vampires are overcome by fatigue at sunup.

"So what can we do for you gentlemen?" Margaret asked.

At the moment, she seemed the strongest of us all, less affected by the dawning day than the rest because of the double-portion blood ration she'd ingested earlier.

"Let's have a seat in the living room, and we'll discuss it." Terry motioned toward the couch and the two chairs facing it.

Taking care to steer clear of the windows, we all headed for the furniture grouping in the center of the room.

Once we were seated, Terry cleared his throat. "So... I know you're wondering why we did what we did, breaking you out of that place. My brother, and my nephew, and my friend Jeff here—they were helping me. I'm dying. I've got aggressive pancreatic cancer, and my doctors tell me I've only got a few months left. Maybe weeks."

Oh no. It was what I'd suspected. He was going to ask us to turn him.

Dread slid down my backbone like an icy breeze. Long before I'd gone to work for Sadie, I'd made a personal pledge not to bite any humans—under any circumstances. It was one of the chief reasons I'd had to leave the vampire sanctuary in Virginia.

It had been easy for me to sign the no-bite agreement required of every vampire who worked at the VHC. Kelly and Heather had signed it too.

Even if they hadn't, they literally weren't capable of turning a human. I might have been—my capabilities hadn't been tested.

In any case, turning someone was a lot more complicated than most humans realized. Of course we couldn't explain to these humans *how* it was actually done—sharing that information was against vampire law.

"I'm not ready to die," he went on. "I want to become like you, a vampire."

"No," I said at the same time Kelly said, "We can't."

"Absolutely not," Margaret added.

Terry's face went from humble to furious in a matter of seconds. "You have to. You owe me."

Glenn stood and towered over us in our seated positions on the sofa. "How can you refuse to help my brother after we saved you?"

"It's illegal," I said.

"The Crimson Accord says it's okay to bite people who give you permission," he argued. "They haven't changed that yet."

"But not to turn them. The law is clear about that," I said.

"Yeah, technically," Jeff said. "But it's not like we're gonna report you. And people do it all the time. A buddy of mine at work fell in love with this vampire lady, and she turned him so they could stay together. What's the big deal? It's in your nature to bite people, right? You'd probably enjoy the hell out of it."

"Not all vampires like biting people, you know," Heather informed him. "We *have* to use blood for nourishment because we *can't* eat food. We all have—"

"Liver failure. I know," Terry said. "I've read the scientific reports. Your bodies can't process food. I have sympathy for you—believe me. I know what it feels like for your body to fail you and drive you to take desperate actions. We wouldn't be here right now if I didn't understand that. So why can't you just help me out?"

For some reason the others looked to me to answer. But what could I say to make these men understand? And to make them let us go?

"I know it must seem like we're being obstinate, but that's not the case. I do appreciate you getting us out of there, and I wish I could help you. I'm sorry you're sick. I truly am. But we can't turn you. We're pacifists."

"So... what... it's like against your religion or something?" he snarled.

"Something like that."

Now Terry turned his frustration on his brother. "Leave it to you to kidnap the only vampires on the planet with morals."

"There are a lot of us actually. Besides, you don't want this life," Margaret said quietly.

"It's better than death," Terry argued.

"Don't be so sure about that," she said. "Especially now. If I'd been given the choice between dying of natural causes and being a vampire, I'd have chosen mortal death."

"That can be arranged," Glenn muttered.

At the veiled threat, Shane, who'd remained quiet until now, spoke up. He stepped away from the wall he'd been leaning against.

"Hey guys, listen, they said they don't want to. It's okay. We'll just find one who does. We'll go out again tomorrow night. We can go into the city. We can pay a prostitute to do it or something."

"No," Terry said quietly. "These vampers owe me. We put ourselves at risk of getting shot or arrested to get them out of that prison camp. We saved their lives. Now one of them is going to save mine—or they're not leaving here."

Casting a nervous glance at my friends then at the sunny window, I stood.

"We'll leave as soon as the sun goes down. We'll sleep in the garage until then. Again, I'm sorry for all the trouble you went to and that we couldn't help you."

Terry stood as well, motioning to Jeff who moved to block the exit door.

"I don't think so. We've got a room for you—right downstairs."

Shane took another step forward, looking bewildered. "What are you talking about? Did you finish out the basement?"

He sounded alarmed, which did nothing to quell the panic rising up my throat.

His uncle gave him a sardonic look. "So to speak. Glenn and I have been doing a little 'remodeling' down there. I think our *guests* will find it comfortable enough."

I did not like the sound of this.

"Really, thank you but there's no need to trouble yourself. We don't need bathrooms or anything. The garage will be fine. At nightfall, we'll just open the door and let ourselves out."

I added an additional apology to try to soothe any lingering sore feelings. "Again, I apologize for all the trouble you went to, and I'm sorry we couldn't help you."

"You mean *wouldn't*." The sickly man sneered. "Put 'em in the basement," he ordered, and the other two older men sprang into action.

Jeff, the largest of the men, wrapped his arms around Heather while Glenn pulled a pistol from his jacket. It was like the one all the guards at the Safety Center carried.

"This is loaded with platinum rounds," he warned. "Just cooperate, and I won't have to use it on any of you."

He grabbed Kelly's upper arm and began steering her toward an open doorway. The top of a stairwell was visible just beyond it.

"No. You can't force us to stay down there," I said and started toward them to try to help my friends.

The time of day and my extreme lack of nutrition had weakened me severely. I had only a fraction of my normal speed and strength.

Terry caught me from behind and jabbed a needle into my neck.

Margaret ran to the home's front door and unlocked it. Before throwing it open, she turned back to look at me. There were tears in her eyes.

"I'm sorry. I can't do this anymore. I can't be a prisoner again."

Then she opened the door and stepped out into the morning light.

"Dammit!" Glenn shouted. "Now we're down to three. Shane, why didn't you stop her?"

The younger guy looked like he was in shock. He stared out the open front door at the pile of ash in the front yard.

"Well, at least shut the damn door. The last thing we need is the busy-body neighbors reporting us," his uncle said.

All the remaining energy deserted my limbs, and my knees buckled. Just before losing consciousness, I heard Shane's voice, loud and anxious.

"Uncle Terry, Glenn—what are you doing? You said they wouldn't be hurt."

And then there was silence and cool blackness.

7

———

HUNGER STRIKE

I woke in a stupor of confusion and pain.

My head was swimming, and my back was sore. When I sat up, I looked around and understood the reason for the back part—we were all lying on a bare concrete floor. The head part I assumed was an effect of the liquid platinum injection.

The substance was sometimes used at the Safety Center to bring unruly inmates under control. Glenn must have pocketed some while at work.

The development of pharmaceutical platinum by a U.S. lab had been the final straw for Imogen.

Saying it was the first step toward trying to remove our rights and eventually eradicate us, she'd left mainstream society and begun living underground full-time, leading her own faction of vampires and preparing them for the resistance movement she believed was inevitable.

Her sister Sadie had countered that it was reasonable for humans, who were at such a physical disadvantage, to want some form of protection against vampires.

Other than the recently developed solar weapons, plat-

35

inum was their only means of defense against vampires who weren't interested in peace between the races.

Before now, I had honestly believed it would only be used against vampire criminals.

But it turned out Imogen was right once again. Suddenly I was struck by a fierce longing for home, for the safety of the Bastion.

If I'd never left, my friends and I would never have been imprisoned. I wouldn't be here now, wondering what these humans would do to us, wondering if this was how I'd meet my final end... and wishing I had one more chance to see Reece and say goodbye.

Beside me, Kelly stirred. "Where are we?"

Her words sounded slurred. Obviously she'd been dosed with platinum as well.

"The basement of Terry's house. We were drugged. They weren't rescuing us—they were kidnapping us."

The good news was there were no windows to admit sunlight. The bad news was there were no windows—or doors—that we could use to make our escape.

It looked as if there might have been a door to an exterior bulkhead at one point, but it had been filled in with cement blocks and mortar. In our weakened states, there was no way we'd be able to break through it.

Even if we did manage it, what if it was daylight outside? I had no idea how long we'd been unconscious or how much time had passed since we'd arrived. It might have been a few hours or a whole day.

"What do you think they plan to do with us?" asked Heather, who'd just awakened as well.

"I'm not sure. But we're going to be okay. I'm going to get us out of here."

My voice sounded so confident, but inside I wasn't as

certain. None of us had taken in blood since we'd left the Safety Center.

We could only go four or five days without it before we began to desiccate. And I wasn't sure how far these men were prepared to go to ensure our cooperation. Would they resort to torture and starvation?

"Maybe we should just bite the old guy," Heather said. "It won't turn him, but they might let us go. They don't know how many bites it takes."

"I doubt they'd release us before they're sure it worked. Besides, that's not who we are—it's not who Sadie taught us to be."

"But Sadie isn't here, is she?" Kelly asked. "And where was she when we were locked up in the Safety Center? I think we should do it. It's worth a try."

"Is it worth your soul?" I asked her. "Is it worth undoing all the progress vampires have made in the world since the Crimson Accord was signed? We have to stay strong, stick to our principles. I'll figure something out."

The door at the top of the stairs opened. We heard the sound of footsteps descending, and I prepared myself for battle. I would not allow myself and my friends to be injected again.

I was a pacifist, but I wasn't a martyr.

It was Glenn. He was armed with a syringe in one hand and the pistol in the other.

He stopped on the bottom step, eyeing us warily. "You ladies ready to be reasonable now? All you have to do is bite him. Do it, and we'll let you go. You gotta be getting thirsty by now."

"Go to hell," Kelly said, but from the corner of my eye I noticed the tips of Heather's fangs slide between her lips.

"We're never going to agree to it," I told him. "Either you

let us go, or you're going to have to carry three dead vampires out of your house."

"No problem. I'll leave you alone for a bit and let you think about it. Meanwhile, I think I'll go get myself a nice, big drink. I sure am thirsty." With a smirk, he added, "Have a nice day."

Marching back up the stairs, he slammed the door behind him. The heavy slide of chains and the click of a padlock followed.

So... we were locked in and on a forced hunger strike.

"I'm beginning to see why some of our kind hate humans," Heather muttered.

"They're not all like that," Kelly reminded her.

Was Shane like that? The alarm in his voice and the concern on his face made me think he was *not* like his uncles and their friend. But he hadn't stopped them either.

No, we were definitely on our own.

Rising to my feet, I said, "Come on. Let's see if we can make any headway with this wall."

8

THE SMELL OF BLOOD

After many hours of bare-finger scratching and digging, we'd made minimal progress on the mortar between the cinderblocks of the recently erected enclosure.

I climbed the stairs to test the door to the kitchen, but it held tight against my efforts to push it open.

Exhausted and dejected, we all lay on the floor again and rested.

Lying with my face against the hard, cold floor, I willed sleep to come. I'd need the energy to continue the excavation project, especially with no blood to replenish my strength.

Unfortunately worry kept me awake. I wasn't sure how long I lay there, thinking of the decisions I'd made that had led me here.

It certainly wasn't what I'd envisioned when my two best friends and I had decided to leave the vampire stronghold and move to Los Angeles to work for Sadie's cause.

"Do you think we'll die in here?" Kelly's voice sounded very small in the quiet of the basement. Obviously, she was having trouble sleeping too.

Overhead, the muffled sound of some sort of sporting event on the television and occasional footsteps could be heard.

It was creepy to think of the humans up there just carrying on with their lives while we were trapped down here.

"No, we won't die. We're going to get out of here," I assured her.

Heather neither agreed nor argued, which worried me. She'd been quiet the whole time as we'd worked and had fallen asleep already.

"Let's just try to get some sleep," I said to Kelly. "I bet we'll break through that wall soon. If not, and it looks like we'll be in here several more days, I'll ask Glenn to bring us some blood bags."

Surely our captors would have to give us some soon. We were no good to them desiccated—unless they'd taken Shane's suggestion.

Maybe they really had gone out and procured some replacement vampires who were more willing.

What would they do with us in that case? Just leave us here and pretend we didn't exist? There was no opportunity to ask because Glenn did not reappear.

"I guess he's waiting for us to get extra-thirsty," Kelly said.

Heather, who was not sleeping after all, held a hand against her grumbling stomach. "Too late. I was already there before we were abducted. Now my mouth feels like Palm Springs, and my belly feels like one of the empty caverns back home."

"I'm actually hallucinating the smell of blood," Kelly said, sounding thoroughly miserable.

I sniffed the air. "I don't think you're hallucinating. I smell it, too."

The three of us got up and began a search of the dark basement. I feared it would end with a gruesome sprung mousetrap.

Instead, when I got to the area where the scent was strongest, my foot struck a cylindrical object and sent it rolling.

"What was that?" Kelly asked.

I dropped to my knees and patted the floor, searching the shadowed corner. "I found it. It's one of those metal water bottles. Glenn must have come in and left it while we were asleep."

"I'm so thirsty I'd settle for water at this point," Heather said.

But when I removed the bottle's top, it was apparent it contained blood. Human blood. I held it out toward Heather.

"You drink first. There's not a lot—maybe half a blood bag—but it'll help."

She took the bottle but hesitated before drinking. "Do you think they poisoned it with platinum?"

"Does it matter at this point? We have to drink something, and we can't get much sicker. The worst that will happen is we'll be knocked out again and wake up with headaches."

She nodded and brought the bottle to her lips, drinking thirstily. She handed it back to me, but I gave it to Kelly. "Your turn."

"You should go first," she said. "There isn't that much here, and I might accidentally drink it all. Your control is better than mine."

Ravenous from spending days without any blood, I didn't argue.

Swirling the bottle to get a feel for how much was left, I took a few swallows then handed it to Kelly.

"Finish it—and then let's get back to work on the mortar."

As we set to work on the wall again, I felt considerably better. My throat was no longer scratchy and hot. The brain fog lifted, and movement came a little easier.

Even Heather seemed to perk up a bit. But the small amount of blood in the bottle didn't last us long.

Pausing a few hours into her digging efforts, Kelly sagged against the cinderblock wall. "My fingers are killing me, and I'm still so friggin' thirsty."

"Me too," I agreed. "But we're making progress."

We'd managed to dig a considerable amount of mortar from between the blocks during this session. Unfortunately there was a lot left. But if we could dislodge one block, the others would come loose more easily. I hoped.

I also hoped there was actually a door on the other side.

"I don't think we can get through it before all our strength is gone," Heather said. "I already feel like I can barely stand."

She paused a beat. "When he comes back, I'm going to tell that bastard I'll bite his brother. At least I'll get some blood out of it—and it might get us out of this basement and upstairs where we'd have a better chance of escaping."

"You can't," I argued, but there was less vehemence in my voice than there had been when I'd made my peace-and-love speech on the first day of our captivity.

"I'll talk to Glenn," I said. "We're not allowed to tell him how turning happens, but maybe I can give him enough information about how it *doesn't* happen that he'll see reason and let us go," I said. "Maybe we can promise to help him find a group of vampires who'll do it."

Or a group who'll teach these guys a lesson.

An image of Reece and his fellow Bloodbound soldiers popped into my mind. They'd take out these weak human men before they even knew what was happening.

I shook off the too-appealing mental picture. Vengeance was never the right path.

And the less I thought of Reece the better. Especially in this weakened and vulnerable state—in this situation where it looked like his philosophy on vampire-human relations was actually the more sensible one.

"Do you think he'll listen to you?" Kelly asked.

"I hope so. Let's not count on it though. We'll take a break then get back to digging. I think a few more hours of work and we should be able to pull out one of those blocks."

We must have all fallen asleep because I woke to the quiet rattle of the door chains followed by soft footsteps descending the staircase.

How long had I slept? Was it day or night? I wasn't sure.

Sitting up, I watched the opening and prepared to reason with Glenn—or attack if necessary.

But it wasn't Glenn who emerged.

It was Shane.

9

HOPE FOR THE FUTURE

He turned one direction then another in the inky darkness. Unlike our eyes, his couldn't see under these conditions.

"Abigail? Are you awake?" he whispered.

"I'm here." I rose and went to him, pulling him to the farthest corner of the basement so as not to awaken Kelly and Heather. "What are you doing here? If they sent you to try to persuade us, it's not going to work."

He kept his voice low. "That's not why I'm here. My uncles don't even know I'm down here. Glenn is at work, and Terry is sleeping. His medication knocks him out. Once he fell asleep, I stole the padlock key."

"Why?"

He hesitated before answering. "If I got you some blood, do you think you would be able to overpower them and escape?"

I nodded. "Do you have access to some?"

"Some, yes, but I'm not sure how much it would take for the three of you to regain your strength."

"We're all low, but about a pint each would really help.

We wouldn't be strong, but we could move enough to get out of here."

Shane's eyebrows lifted and he blew out a long breath. "That's a lot. What about for just you?"

"I'm not leaving my friends," I answered immediately. "Why are you even offering to help us escape?"

"This is not what I signed up for. I love my Uncle Terry, and I owe him for taking me in after my parents... well... I owe him. But this is wrong."

He gestured to indicate our basement prison.

"I've tried to talk to him, but he won't listen. He's desperate. The doctors have told him he's got only weeks left to live, if that long. He plans to keep you down here until you're thirsty enough to give in and do it. And Glenn's talking about shortening the time frame by threatening to push all of you out into the sun tomorrow morning. He'll be driving here tonight after he gets off work. I don't *think* he'd really daylight you, but I don't know for sure. Terry wasn't doing too hot today, and Glenn's really worried about him. There's a chance he'll follow through and decide to start from scratch with some willing vampires."

"Well if he's planning to start from scratch, maybe he'll release us."

Shane shook his head in a definitive way. "No. He won't. He's afraid if you don't willingly participate, you might identify them to the police and press charges. Kidnapping is still illegal, you know, even kidnapping vampires, thanks to the Accord. I think escape is the only answer. You have to run—tonight. To do that, you'll need blood."

I thought about it for a few moments. He was right. These weren't reasonable men.

No amount of talking would convince them. And I had

no interest in sticking around to find out if Glenn would carry out his daylighting plan.

"Okay. You said you had access to some blood?"

Shane nodded. Then he slowly lifted his arm toward me, pushing up his sleeve and exposing the inside of his elbow.

There was a bandage over it, and underneath, a fairly fresh cut.

The blood in that water bottle hadn't come from a blood bag. It had come from Shane.

I staggered backward, shuddering with a blend of revulsion and unholy temptation. "No. I can't. I won't drink from you."

"It's okay," he said. "I know I won't turn from being bitten one time."

"What makes you say that?"

He shrugged, and another surge of tempting blood warmed his cheek. "I just know, okay? It takes more exposure to the venom than that, so I'm not worried."

"I still can't do it."

"Can't you just put the vow on hold for a night? I mean, this must qualify as special circumstances, right?"

"It does... but there's a reason I made that vow."

I hesitated. There was no way I could explain to this human about my unusual vampire heritage, that I might be able to turn a human with a single bite—or about what had happened with Josiah and how I'd vowed to never let it happen again.

Shane was offering to help us in our hour of need. He was offering his own blood. Maybe he deserved honesty—but I simply couldn't give it to him.

"For some of us, drinking blood is more than sustenance. It's... a problem," I said.

That much was true. I went on with my fabricated excuse.

"You know how some people can drink alcohol or even do drugs recreationally and they don't become addicted? While others do?"

He nodded. "Yeah. My Uncle Glenn stopped drinking because he said it got to where if he had one drink he'd have fifteen and wake up with no memory of where he'd been or what he'd done the night before."

"Exactly. Well, blood is like that for some vampires."

That was also true. Not for me personally, but I *had* met several recovering blood addicts during my time at the VHA. Kelly was one as well.

It was a plausible reason not to drink from the vein—one Shane could understand.

"Maybe it's an addiction gene they had while human or something, no one knows," I said. "But for some vampires it's addictive. It's impossible for us to follow a twelve-step program or go to rehab because we can't avoid drinking blood altogether. We have to have it to survive. It's literally the only form of nutrition our bodies will accept. We can't digest food or any other liquid—our bodies absorb the blood we drink directly."

"So you're an addict. And yet you're forced to be around the source of your addiction every day."

"Yes," I lied. "Like I said, no one knows why. I have no way of knowing if it's genetic because no one in my family drank or did drugs. But when I was first turned, it became obvious pretty quickly that I didn't need to be drinking directly from people."

"What about your friends?"

"Same story. Maybe that's why the three of us were attracted to the Vampire-Human Coalition. It offered us a way to give back, to try to make up for the damage we'd done before getting our thirst under control. That's why I can't bite you. The vow is more than a belief system. It's a safety net. If I were to try it... it would be my first time drinking from a human in more than a year. I'm not sure what would happen. I might not be able to stop."

"Wow. I never would have guessed. You seem so..."

"Civilized?" I finished his sentence for him. "Harmless? Never forget the original source of vampirism was a powerful wild animal infected by killer bees. That animalistic instinct paired with a thirst for blood means none of us is truly civilized. One of the many reasons we refused to turn your uncle."

"Okay well, whether you drink my blood or not, we have to get you all out of here tonight—*before* Glenn gets here." He paused a beat to think. "If you're too weak to run, you could take Terry's SUV."

"I can't drive."

"What? You look old enough to have a license."

"I am. I was seventeen when I was turned. But I never got a license. My family... didn't have a car."

That was the simple explanation. We didn't have time to get into the rest of it.

"Heather's too sick to drive, but maybe Kelly could do it. I'll wake them. What time is it?"

"About three o'clock. A couple hours till sunset. I'll get the keys. Glenn won't be here until about seven. You can just wait in the garage until the sun sets and it's safe to go out."

Shane ran up the steps and out of sight. I roused my friends, encouraging them to get on their feet and get moving.

After dark we'd drive straight to Los Angeles, to Sadie's

headquarters. She'd know what to do. If anyone could help with our legal troubles it was her.

"What's going on?" Kelly asked.

"We're getting out of here. Shane is helping us. Now come on and be quiet."

Heather was more difficult to rouse.

"Go 'way," she mumbled, swatting at my hand on her shoulder. "Tired."

She really needed blood. Her hypoglycemia had progressed to the point she was confused and irritable. As soon as we got on the road, I'd have to locate some blood bags for her.

Her continued lethargy was concerning to say the least.

Shane met us at the top of the stairs, holding a set of keys and several blankets. "I thought these might come in handy in case you have to sleep in the car or something. You could use it to cover the windows and block out the sun."

"Good thinking. Thanks," I said, taking them from him.

Since we were only going to LA, which was about a six-hour drive, we wouldn't be needing them. We could easily make it there before sunrise, but I didn't want to clue him into our plans.

Shane stuffed his fingertips into his pockets and rocked forward and back on his feet. His pensive expression struggled to become a sad smile.

"Okay, well, I guess it's goodbye then. I'll stay here and keep watch. If Uncle Terry wakes up, I'll distract him and get him whatever he needs, keep him away from the garage until tonight when you're long gone. You should have a good head start before he notices his car is missing."

We headed for the door connecting the kitchen and the garage. My friends went through it, but I stopped just short of the opening and turned back to face Shane. "Thank you."

"Don't mention it—please. I feel terrible I played a part in getting you into this mess. If I'd known they were planning to hold you prisoner..."

"I know," I said, brushing off his apology. "And ultimately, you probably saved our lives by getting us out of that detention center. I'm glad I met you, Shane. Humans like you give me hope for the future."

"I'm glad I met you too. I wish... I mean, if you ever need anything... well, you know where to find me."

Without planning it or even thinking, I leaned forward and placed a swift kiss on his cheek. He smelled good, like woodsmoke and spice. And fresh blood.

Drawing back sharply, I swallowed hard and pressed my fingernails into my palms to suppress a sudden craving.

"Don't worry about us. And thank you again. We'll call the authorities and report an abandoned car wherever we leave it, so your uncle is sure to get it back."

Then I stepped into the garage and stopped—in shock.

Glenn was there with a hand on each of my friends' necks.

10

BLOOD LUST

He'd used a pair of platinum handcuffs to lock them together. Further weakened by the rare metal, Heather looked like she might drop to the garage floor and drag Kelly down with her.

Worse, Glenn's truck was parked in the driveway outside the open garage door, directly behind the SUV. Even if I could somehow grab my friends and get them into the SUV, our path to escape was blocked.

When he saw Shane, Glenn let out a mocking laugh. "*You* let the vamps out? She's used her powers on you, boy—mesmerized you. I *told* you to stay away from that basement."

"Glenn... what are you doing here? I thought you were working today," Shane said.

"I'll bet you did," the guard said with a sneer. "I took off a half day so I could check on Terry, and it's a good thing I did. Oh well, no matter. Now I don't have to bother dragging your scrawny corpses up from the basement. I can just walk you right out the front into the sunlight—unless you've changed your minds about turning my brother."

Dragging my two friends along with him, he took several steps toward the open garage door. The sun was still up and strong enough to do plenty of damage if not kill them outright.

"Last chance..." He jerked them toward the light in a joking-not-joking false start and actually *laughed*.

We'd all endured insults and small aggressions during our time at the Safety Center—even before that. It was part of the vampire life.

It could be tolerated with enough practice and patience. But I'd never had someone I loved threatened with daylighting.

What happened next felt like a blur of sight, sound, and sensation. I was on him before even realizing I was planning to attack.

Actually, there was no plan, only instinct. I simply could *not* let this man hurt my friends—I had to stop him.

I grabbed the front of his uniform, pulling him away from Kelly and Heather. Clearly shocked by my speed and sudden nearness, he flailed and stumbled backward, grabbing onto the pendant necklace I always wore and breaking the chain.

He looked down at his palm. "What is this? Some kind of vampire weapon?"

Thrusting the pendant's pointed tip out toward me, he waved it in my face as if wielding a dagger.

"You stay back, or I'll cut you with it."

"Give that back," I growled, feeling my fangs protrude.

Glenn was dead wrong about the artifact he was holding. It wasn't a weapon, and it certainly couldn't kill me, but I wasn't going to explain its significance.

Someone like him could never understand.

He snickered. "Oh, I don't think so. Shoe's on the other foot now, isn't it, leech?"

Advancing toward me, he made a few weak jabs in my direction. His hand shook so hard he almost dropped the necklace. In fact, it slipped from his grip.

Only the chain wrapped around his wrist saved the glass orb in its hilt from smashing on the hard garage floor.

If he breaks it, I'll kill him.

No. All life is precious—even his.

I worked to calm my tone and my predator's instincts. "I won't hurt you. There's no need for this. Just give my necklace back and let us go."

"You think I'm stupid? You'll report me and Terry to the police. We'll be arrested. I'll lose my job."

"I won't," I told him honestly.

All I wanted was to get my pendant back and get my friends out of here safely. "I promise—just give me back the necklace, move your truck out of the way, and we'll drive out of here in Terry's SUV. You'll never see us or hear from us again."

"Yeah right. Now you're trying to play your mind tricks on me. Well it's not going to work. All you vamps are liars and hypnotists, but I'm too smart for you."

Keeping the pendant's sharp tip pointed at me, he fished in his pocket with the other hand, managing to extract his phone.

"I'll call the police *myself.* I'll tell them you three took me hostage at the Safety Center and forced me to bring you here. Who do you think they'll believe, huh? Me or you?"

There was motion in my peripheral vision, and then Glenn was falling. With no chance to brace himself, his head impacted the garage floor with a loud thud. A dark pool of liquid seeped out from beneath it.

"No," I screamed, knowing what would come next. Kelly and Heather had used their linked arms to knock him off his feet.

Now both fell to their knees and began drinking the spilled blood. It took only moments for them to move to Glenn himself.

"No," I repeated, charging forward and pulling them away from the fallen man.

It wasn't easy. Blood lust had set in. Because we'd been deprived for several days, it was even more severe than usual.

Picture trying to take a food bowl away from a starving dog while he's eating—then multiply it by about a thousand.

Still handcuffed together, my friends growled and swiped at me with their free hands, struggling to get back to the source of that life-saving, energizing blood.

I wasn't angry with them—I understood completely. The scent of the fresh blood was nearly driving me mad as well.

But this was bad. Very bad. Glenn was a Safety Center guard, and he was dying if not dead already.

When he was discovered, the police really would think we'd kidnapped him and killed him.

And now neither Kelly nor Heather could drive—not only would they have zero interest in leaving the feast, but they'd be intoxicated for hours.

Dashing a desperate glance over at Shane, I barked an order. "Get his keys. You're going to drive us."

11

DANGER AHEAD

Shane looked like he might be in shock. Remaining motionless, he stared at his uncle bleeding out on the floor.

"Shane," I yelled, and finally he looked at me. "You have to drive, and I need to get their handcuffs off. Get his keys. Now."

He still didn't move. His gaze shifted from his uncle's body to me. His eyes were wide with terror, which made sense, but I had no time for reassurances or kid gloves.

The garage door was wide open. A neighbor could have seen what just happened and called the police to report a band of "savage" vampires roaming their peaceful neighborhood and murdering their "upstanding" neighbor.

We might have mere minutes before a Vampire Suppression Unit showed up armed with the latest in anti-vamp ultraviolet and platinum weapons.

I went to Shane, touching his shoulder and speaking in a low, serious voice. "We have to go—now. Your Uncle Terry could wake up any minute and come out here."

Swallowing hard, I added, "I'd hate to have to hurt him. Or you."

In all honesty I had no interest in harming the sickly man, and the thought of attacking Shane turned my stomach. But we were out of time. I had to say something to snap him out of his stunned inertia.

"The keys..." he finally said.

"Yes. We need them. Now move it. Get us out of here and I'll let you go. Refuse to help us and I promise you'll be sorry."

Apparently falling for my bluff—he had no idea what I was, or wasn't, capable of—Shane began moving, walking over to his uncle and retrieving the keys he'd dropped.

"The necklace too," I said, reluctant to go any closer to the bleeding man.

Shane obeyed then looked to me for further orders.

"Unlock the handcuffs first. Then pick up the blankets," I instructed. "Get them and put them around us."

There was no way I could restrain Kelly and Heather from fully draining Glenn while also draping the three of us to protect us from the light of day outside.

We wouldn't burst into flame immediately between the garage and the truck, but we'd be badly burned, and it would require even more blood to heal.

That would be dangerous for Shane as the only human within reach. We'd be in close quarters in the truck's cab, but there was no choice now. We couldn't wait around here —we had to leave, and he *had* to drive us.

He obeyed without a word, grabbing the blankets from the garage floor and draping them around us.

"Now open the rear door of the truck and come back. You're going to close the garage door behind us then get in the driver's seat."

"Where are we going?" he asked in a dead-sounding voice.

"I'll tell you when we get on the road."

Wherever we went, it needed to be close. The blankets could only do so much. We needed to find shelter.

Once we were covered, I moved toward the truck just outside the garage, pulling my unwilling friends along with me. Neither of them was very large, but they'd just fed, so the short journey was a struggle.

The truck's driver's side door slammed behind Shane, and I had a moment of panic. He had the key fob. If he chose to, he could simply hit the lock button and drive away, leaving us behind to be arrested when the police arrived.

But he didn't. He started the engine and waited for me to get my friends into the backseat before pulling out of the driveway. I tented a blanket over my face and peeked from the opening to look through the windshield.

Shane drove out of the driveway and to the end of the neighborhood street. "Where do you want to go?"

"Take us into the city," I said. "You can drop us off there and come back home."

He nodded and took a left, following signs toward a highway onramp.

"You think he'll turn?" he asked in a small voice, glancing back over his shoulder.

"Your uncle?" *Oh no.* "Why? Has he been bitten before? By whom? How many times?"

"I don't know. At least a few. At work. Hazard of the job, you know?"

So that was how Shane had known a single bite wouldn't turn him. I certainly hoped Glenn did *not* turn. If he did, he'd more than likely come after us. But that was another problem for another day.

"Give me the key ring and the necklace," I said, still trying to maintain an intimidating tone.

It felt wrong to keep frightening Shane and ordering him around, especially after he'd released us from the basement prison and given us his own blood to drink.

But if I didn't keep him scared, he might drive to a police station—or maybe even pull over to the shoulder of the road, get out, and just leave us there.

I had to keep him under my control at least until the sun set.

Unfortunately, his uncle had been wrong—we didn't possess mind control powers. If we did, we'd have left the Safety Center long ago.

Shane followed my instructions, handing the items to me then pulling the truck onto the highway. It was packed because of rush hour, and he stayed quiet as he navigated traffic.

I set to work mending my necklace. Thankfully the link that had stretched open when Glenn yanked it from my neck hadn't snapped—it was only bent out of shape. I reattached it to its neighboring link and pressed the silver back into shape to lock them together.

Then I draped the pendant around my neck again, feeling instantly better with it resting in its usual spot against my sternum.

When we reached the San Francisco city limits, Shane finally spoke again. His voice was tense. The full impact of what he'd seen had probably registered now that the shock of seeing his uncle die was wearing off.

"Do you know where to find shelter?"

Like I'd actually *tell* him where we would be hiding out.

Yes, he'd been decent to us during this whole horrendous experience. He'd wanted to help us escape.

But that was before we'd killed his uncle in front of his eyes. Chances were good he was feeling a whole lot less charitable toward us now.

"It's not your concern. Just get us to Nob Hill. I'll give you turn by turn directions from there."

If only the sun had set already. While it was up, I had to fight daytime drowsiness. A few times during the drive, I nodded off and jerked awake again.

If I were to fall soundly asleep like my friends, there was no reason to believe Shane *wouldn't* drive to a police station and deliver the three of us like a neatly wrapped gift box.

When we reached Sutter Street, I leaned forward a bit to give him instructions. "Okay, try to find a spot somewhere along here."

We both kept our eyes peeled as we cruised past classic brick and terra cotta buildings, glass office towers, street-level eateries, and a beautiful art deco hotel.

When my friend Larkin's apartment building came into sight, I was thrilled—and a bit shocked to be honest—to see an open metered spot in front of it.

"There," I practically yelled, pointing to it.

"I see it." Shane maneuvered into the spot and parked.

Larkin and I had become close friends when we'd both lived in LA. I'd visited her in San Francisco many times after she'd moved here.

Naturally I hadn't had the opportunity to call her since getting out of the Safety Center, but I knew she'd help us. Maybe she'd even lend us her car for the trip to LA. It was outfitted with sunshields and surround-view cameras for daytime driving.

"We'll get out here," I said. "It's a few blocks away."

"I'll help you with them," he said.

"No. No thank you. I can handle it."

My plan was to cover my friends and myself with the blankets, watch Shane drive away, then dash inside the apartment building and drag Kelly and Heather to the elevator. Somehow.

He peered into the back seat. "How? They're dead asleep, and you're about to pass out yourself. I know you're strong, but you can't carry them both. The sun's still up. Your blankets could slip or something."

At that moment, the sun came out from behind a cloud and cast brilliant golden rays down on the street and side-walk around us.

It might as well have been a flashing neon sign reading "Danger Ahead."

My gaze bounced from Shane's face to the apartment building's sliding front doors and back to him. He was right. And the more I thought about it, the more I realized how stupid it would be of me to allow him to drive away.

He could go directly to a police station and tell them about his uncle's death—and exactly where he'd dropped off the vampires responsible for it.

I had to be smart about this. We were no longer respectable VHC employees. We weren't run of the mill vampires. We were escapees, and now we'd murdered a human. Well, it was self-defense, but no one would believe that.

The police might already be looking for three vampires who fit our descriptions. There was a chance Terry's neighbors *had* seen us—or that he'd awakened and found his brother's body.

I heaved a resigned sigh. "Okay, you're right. I need help getting them into the building."

Shane rolled his eyes. "Duh. Just tell me which one it is."

He must have read my wary expression because he

added, "I'm not going to turn you in, Abigail. I never wanted any of this to happen. And I know what happened to Glenn wasn't your fault. Or theirs. He held you prisoner. He starved you. You can trust me."

Could I?

It looked like I had no other choice.

12

——————

TOO LATE

Shane got out of the truck and opened the back door, tugging one of the blankets around me to make sure I was thoroughly covered.

"You go ahead and get out. I'll help them," he said.

"They may not be able to wake up. Carrying both at once is going to be tough."

He grinned at me. "Then it's a good thing I work out every day. You never know when you might need to lift a couple of sacked-out vamps. At least they're little ones. Some of the males I've seen I probably wouldn't be able to budge. I'm not sure if they were that way before they turned, or if it happens when they vamp out, but there are some scary-big bastards running around out there."

Reece, with his six-four height and his two hundred pounds of solid muscle, came immediately to mind.

At the moment, I wasn't really interested in discussing large vampire males. I was hoping the six-foot human one with me now could manage to finish what he'd started and wouldn't yell for help the minute we were exposed.

Carefully lifting first Kelly, then Heather, Shane stood

and moved away from the truck, carrying their wrapped bodies one over each shoulder. I followed, casting wary glances at the pedestrians I could see through the opening in my blanket-drape.

Maybe they'd think Shane was a rug delivery man or something. It wasn't commonplace to see vampires out before dark.

"Where to?" he asked as I caught up to him.

"Right here." I headed toward the apartment building's front doors, clutching my blanket tightly around me.

After we'd stepped through the sliders, he gave me a sardonic look. "I thought you said it was a few blocks away."

I shrugged and went to the elevator to push the call button. The doors opened, and we stepped inside.

What Shane had said in the truck was true. I *was* about to pass out. The lack of rations was really catching up with me. In fact, I had to lean against the elevator car's interior on the way up to the ninth floor.

A ding sounded, and the doors slid open.

This was where I had to make a decision. Even if it took a couple of trips, I could manage to get my friends down the long, carpeted hallway and into Larkin's apartment without Shane's help. I *could* let him leave.

But at this point, the police had no idea where we were. Shane *did*.

Which meant I shouldn't let him go quite yet.

He didn't even ask if I wanted him to come along, just followed me out of the elevator and down the hall to Larkin's door. The building was quiet—a lot of vampires lived here, and they were no doubt just waking up from their daytime sleep.

Like the rest of us, Larkin worked at night. She'd be

home now, though knowing her, she was probably still snoozing.

"Is this your place?" Shane asked.

He was still holding my two unconscious friends, and the strain was beginning to show on his face. There was a light sheen of perspiration on his forehead and upper lip from the exertion.

A swell of gratitude mixed with despair. *What* was I going to do with him?

"No. It belongs to my friend."

I knocked on the door, anticipating Larkin's surprise and really looking forward to seeing her friendly face. Of course we wouldn't have time for a real catch-up visit—I didn't want her to get in trouble for harboring wanted criminals or something.

We just needed a safe place and a little time to regroup. And we couldn't start our trip to Los Angeles until the sun went down and my two friends sobered up—and until we found some discreet transportation. A stolen prison guard's truck wasn't the ideal choice.

When there was no answer at the door, I rang the door-bell. Still nothing.

"Maybe she's not home?" Shane suggested.

"Maybe. I mean, she didn't have a boyfriend last time we talked but it's been a month since then—maybe six weeks. The good news is she keeps a spare key right..."

I flipped up the front panel of a decorative wall hanging to one side of Larkin's door and removed the key from its hiding place. "...here."

"I used it last time I visited," I explained. "My plane arrived a little early, and she was still at the—"

Here I stopped. Larkin might not want me sharing information about her current employment status with a stranger. She found the job a little embarrassing.

Once, she'd had a prestigious position as a researcher with the Center for Hematology and Liver Disorders. But then her human employer had gotten nervous about having a vampire working around such important blood samples and fired her.

His fear must have been a common one or highly contagious because she'd been unable to locate another job in her specialty—or in any other scientific capacity.

When her savings had run out, she'd done what so many others of us in her position had done—swallowed her pride and taken whatever work she could get.

"... still at work," I finished my sentence generically for Shane's sake then turned the key in the lock and opened the door.

The first thing I noticed was the stale air. Larkin was a big fan of opening the windows and letting in the fresh air —day or night, year round.

"Something's wrong," I said to Shane as we moved into the apartment and he lay first Kelly then Heather on the long, red leather sofa. "She's not here."

He turned and did a visual scan of the room. "How do you know? Maybe she's just sleeping and didn't hear us?"

"No. I'd be able to sense her. The apartment's empty." I walked over and swiped a fingertip through the dust atop one of the side tables. Larkin was also a neat freak. "She hasn't been here for a long time."

A rapid pulse tapped the inside of my neck. Where could she be?

There was a small possibility the restaurant where she worked had put her on the dayshift—it had no exterior windows—but that was unlikely. The primary benefit of hiring vampirish workers was having the nightshift covered with no complaints.

Even if she *was* at work, that didn't explain the dusty furniture and stale air. I whirled around, searching the room, then ran into the kitchen.

No food bowl on the floor. No Drak.

That settled it. And settled my nerves a bit.

"I think she must have gone away on a trip. Her dog, Drak, isn't here." Bending to check the lower cabinet closest to the refrigerator, I added, "His food's gone. The water and food bowls too."

"Could she have moved out?" Shane asked. "Maybe the new tenant didn't know about the spare key?"

"No. These are her things."

I walked over to her fireplace mantel and picked up a framed photo of the two of us, offering it to him. "See? This was taken last year in Los Angeles. Her name's Larkin."

He studied the picture. "She's beautiful." Glancing up to meet my eyes he added, "You look like you could be sisters."

I turned away to hide my embarrassment at his compliment. Vampires were still capable of blushing.

"No. Just friends. She was the first friend I made when I moved to California. She showed me around, taught me about living in a big city."

He snickered. "You were a country mouse, huh?"

"That's an understatement. Larkin's the total opposite. She grew up here in San Francisco before... you know, turning. We were neighbors in LA before she moved back here."

"Cool. So, I assume she won't mind you all staying here? You should probably lie low until I find out whether Uncle Terry's found Glenn's body and reported the attack."

"I'm really sorry about that," I said. "Kelly and Heather

were so thirsty they couldn't stop themselves. They're pacifists like me. None of us meant for him to end up dead."

He nodded. "I know. Glenn brought it on himself. He's always been a little rough—he and Uncle Terry. I never imagined they'd become kidnappers, though. Or be violent."

"Well, Glenn's nickname at the Safety Center was 'Clubber.' People said he used to walk around swinging this baton, and he'd swing it for the least infraction."

"Wow." Shane blew out a breath. "That's awful. I wish more people knew what was really going on in those places."

"Do you think it would change things? Do you really think the humans would care?"

"I care," he said.

"Well, from what I'm seeing lately, you're the exception."

Shane looked around and shifted from one foot to the next. His voice held a note of nervousness.

"So, I guess I should go. Probably shouldn't leave the truck parked outside the building in case Uncle Terry did wake up and call the police."

Ugh. He was right about the truck. But I couldn't let him leave yet. I looked around as well.

Was there a room I could lock him in until we were safely away from the city? I'd have to wake one of my friends and have her move the truck as soon as night fell and it was safe to go out. When we left the apartment, we'd leave the keys here for Shane as well as a note telling him where to find it.

Before I could make up my mind, he drew his phone from his pocket—I hadn't realized he had one on him— which was dumb.

He checked the screen, and his eyelids widened. Then his jaw dropped. "Crap. It's too late."

"What do you mean? There's an alert out on the truck already?" A vivid image of police cruisers surrounding the building filled my mind's eye.

"Worse."

He turned the screen around toward me. And I saw *my* face.

Heather and Kelly's pictures were there too—along with all three of our names and a terrifying headline.

13

CALLING A FRIEND

The caption beneath the photos read: *Vampires escape Safety Center in bloody rampage that leaves six guards dead.*

It was hard to breathe as I skimmed the article that followed. Apparently, the official story was that the three of us had *orchestrated* the breakout.

It mentioned Glenn was a guard at the Center and speculated that we'd overpowered him, forcing him to deactivate the western fence, then taken him along as a hostage, killing him and stealing his truck when we'd made it to freedom.

The report cautioned that we were to be considered highly dangerous repeat offenders and gave a hotline number, asking for any information regarding our whereabouts.

The only good news was that very few of the vampires who'd fled the Center had been recaptured. If there really had been an order to exterminate them, they'd escaped just in time.

"None of it's true," Shane said, dismay coloring his tone.

"It doesn't matter. They'll shoot us on sight."

Any hope I'd ever entertained of clearing my name and returning to my old life, my old job, and my friends—vanished in that instant.

"I'll tell them the truth," Shane vowed.

I shook my head. "They'll just assume you've been mesmerized, that you're saying what we told you to say. Who would believe you'd actually assist a group of 'highly dangerous' vampires willingly? Especially now that your uncle is dead and covered in fang marks?"

"I *am* willing to help you. I got you out of that basement. I got you here, right?"

"Yes, but you believed I'd hurt you if you didn't."

He grinned. "I'm not afraid of you. You're a pacifist, remember?"

Nodding toward my friends, I said, "So were they until our lives were threatened and they were deprived of blood for too long. Never forget what we are. None of us is very far from our animal nature."

He gave me an alert glance, perhaps regarding me as a threat at long last.

"Well... what are you going to do now? I mean I can go down and move the truck, but even then you won't be able to stay here long. The sidewalk was crowded with people when we came in. Someone might have seen the blankets and those bright yellow pants and suspected something. Someone could see this bulletin and call it in. I don't think you can stay in the city tonight."

"Wasn't planning to. We're going to leave as soon as it's dark."

"How?"

"That's a good question. I was hoping to borrow Larkin's car, but obviously she's not here, so I doubt her car is. Thanks to that alert, the authorities will be watching the airports and train stations—bus stations too."

"Do you even have money or a credit card for tickets?" Shane asked. "I would guess your personal belongings like wallets and purses and stuff are back at the Safety Center."

"You're right. I'll need to stop by the—oh no." I closed my eyes, my hands coming up to cover my nose and mouth in a steeple as it hit me.

"What?"

I had been about to say the word *bank*, but that was hopeless as well. "I'm sure they've frozen our accounts."

This was so bad. How *were* we going to travel? We had no money for transportation or to buy blood bags.

"Can I use your phone?" I asked.

"Sure. You have another friend here in town with a car?"

"No. Not in town. But I am calling a friend who'll know what to do."

Sadie Aldritch was the only vampire I knew with enough clout to help us. Well, not the *only* one but the only one I'd be willing to ask.

I knew both her numbers by heart—her personal phone and her office at the Vampire-Human Coalition.

No one picked up at either. The call to her cell number went right to voicemail.

Which was weird. She was practically fused to her phone. She got calls from important vampires and humans from around the world on a daily basis.

When I called the VHC, it rang a few times then went to an automated voice recording with instructions on how to reach the various departments. Even pressing zero sent me to a recording inviting me to leave a message.

Assuming the police would be checking all VHC communications for word on the "escapees," I declined to leave one. Ending the call, I started to hand the phone back to Shane.

A frightening new possibility stopped me mid-motion. "Do you think they could track you here with this device?"

His eyelids widened. "Oh man. Probably. Maybe I should take out the battery?"

As he reached for the phone, I crushed it, shattering the screen and dropping jagged pieces of black plastic to the floor.

"Oh," he said in surprise. "Well, okay then."

"I'm sorry. I can't afford to take any chances."

"Don't worry about it. I have insurance on it. I just hope they didn't run a trace on it already. You should get out of here—soon. That's assuming you can even hire a car without a credit card—or without being recognized and turned in. The article said there was a reward. I wish there was a way you could, you know, blend in. But with your eyes..."

His voice trailed off, and he shrugged in a way that told me he hoped what he'd said wasn't offensive. "I mean I think the lilac is pretty, but—"

"Blend in," I practically shouted, interrupting him. "That's it! Oh, I hope Larkin only packed for a short trip."

Rushing from the kitchen-living room area to Larkin's bedroom and into the connected bathroom, I rummaged through the vanity drawers, hoping to find some of the "props" she used for her job.

Yes. She'd left a variety of cosmetics and a large supply of colored contact lenses.

Heather, Kelly, and I would disguise ourselves as humans, using the contacts to cover our tell-tale lilac eyes. Larkin's work makeup and clothing would further obscure our natural appearance and make us look less like our mug shots.

Going to her closet next, I threw it open and sorted through the garments she'd left behind.

Sadly, she'd taken all of her normal clothing, leaving only the skimpier items that fit the much-despised dress code for her job.

Oh well, beggars couldn't be choosers. Maybe it was for the best. If people didn't look too closely at our faces, they'd be less likely to match them to the photos and descriptions being circulated by the police.

This *was* downtown San Francisco after all. We'd fit in instead of standing out. We could walk out of the building and right through the city streets without turning a head.

I pulled out a few items and turned to toss them on the bedspread. Shane had followed me. He was leaning against the bedroom door frame, grinning.

"Disguises huh? Those are some... interesting clothes your friend owns."

One of his eyebrows lifted as he surveyed the micro-dresses and midriff-baring tops and teeny weeny hot-shorts Larkin was required to wear on the job.

"What does she... do?"

"She's a waitress. At Fangers."

The campy themed restaurant was something along the lines of Hooters, only the beautiful female employees were all vampires instead of busty human babes. We used to roll our eyes at the chain's slogan—"Burgers with Bite. Open All Night."

She hated working there, but the tips were as large as the outfits were small, and she needed the money.

"I've never been there, but maybe I *should* go. I'm sure

you'll look great in this," he drawled, picking up a tiny halter top.

I snatched it away from him. "I'm sure *you'll* never know."

Scurrying from the room, I went to wake my friends. After I explained where we were and what the plan was, they went into the bathroom to change out of their prison uniforms and apply their streetwalker disguises.

I would change into mine after I'd dealt with Shane. I knew what I had to do now. There was no other choice.

The police were looking for us, and he was a witness.

14

———

SOMETHING YOU SHOULD KNOW

For the second time in one day, I was telling Shane goodbye. *This* time it would be for good.

"So," I said to him, feeling heartsick.

"So..." He wore a tight-lipped expression, and his eyes were troubled. "I guess this is where you tell me to get lost."

I gave him a sad smile in return. "This is where I tell you 'thank you.' Thanks for being one of the good guys. I hope you don't get in too much trouble for helping us."

His lips quirked, and he reached out to brush a loose curl behind my ear. "I was mesmerized, remember? I couldn't resist if I wanted to."

The unexpected intimacy of the gesture sent a shiver through me. I moved back and let out an uncomfortable giggle. "Really, don't be a hero when you talk to them, okay? Lie and say we forced you to come with us. They'll believe it."

He frowned. "I hate to leave without knowing you'll be okay."

Guilt assaulted me. *We* would be leaving, but he wouldn't.

75

"Don't worry about us," I mumbled. "We'll work something out."

"I *am* worried. I've got a little money I could give you." Shane pulled his wallet from his back jeans pocket.

The guilt tripled. I held up a hand and shook my head. "That's nice of you, but I can't kill your phone *and* take your money."

"You can, and you will. You have to. It's the least I can do."

Removing all the cash, he pressed it into my hand.

"It's enough for some blood bags and an Uber out of town. Unfortunately not enough if you're planning to go too *far* out of town, but at least it'll give you a head start."

"Thank you," I said again, my breath quickening and a lump growing in my throat. Suddenly I felt sad about the prospect of doing what I had to do. "Well, it certainly hasn't been boring."

"Definitely not. I'll never forget you. And I'll probably worry about you every day for forever. I wish I knew you were going to be okay."

"We will be," I blurted.

And please stop being so nice. This is hard enough as it is.

"We have friends in high places—well, one friend in high places. She'll be able to help us."

I wouldn't tell him we were headed to Los Angeles. For all our sakes it was best for Shane to have no idea where we'd gone.

Even if he *didn't* intend to betray us—and I was pretty sure he didn't—the police had ways of getting information out of people.

Just then Heather and Kelly emerged from the bathroom looking human, thanks to the contact lenses, and *very* sexy, thanks to Larkin's work wardrobe.

They were both laughing.

"Can you imagine what Sadie's gonna say when we show up looking like this?" Heather asked.

Kelly and I shushed her simultaneously, but from the look on Shane's face it was too late. He'd heard her, and he knew who she was talking about.

"Sadie Aldritch? The Vampire-Human Coalition leader? Is that where you're planning to go—to her?"

Great. Nice moment over. Now I definitely had no choice.

"I'm sorry about this." Pushing Shane into the bathroom, I shut the door between us and bent the knob to one side so it could no longer be turned.

"Hey!" He jiggled it then banged on the door. "Abbi, what are you doing? Why did you do that?"

"I'm sorry, but like I said, we can't take any chances. I'll let someone know where to find you as soon as we're safely away. You won't be in there long."

"Wait. There's something you should know," he yelled through the door. "There's been a bombing. In Los Angeles. At the VHC headquarters. It happened last night. I saw it on my phone. The terrorists took out the whole building. A bunch of the vampires who worked there were killed. They said on the news that they're trying to figure out if Sadie Aldritch was one of them."

"Oh my God," Heather said in a hushed voice.

"I can't believe it." Kelly turned to me, her eyes huge. "Do you think he's telling the truth?"

I ran into the living room, grabbed the TV remote, and searched channels until I found a news station. There it was, a story about the bombing, complete with horrific live video coverage of smoldering rubble and gawking onlookers.

"Oh no," I breathed.

"It's true," Kelly said with tears in her eyes.

Heather sounded choked up as well. "All those people. All our friends." She stared at the screen with one hand covering her mouth.

"Maybe they got out," I said, but the video of the scene looked like a war zone. I didn't know how anyone—vampire or human—could have survived it.

"Do you think Sadie was there?" Kelly whispered.

A bolt of fear rocked my heart. "God, I hope not."

Had Sadie been in her office when the bomb went off? There was a chance she hadn't been.

Since I'd been out of touch for the past few weeks while under incarceration, I wasn't sure if she was even in Los Angeles. She did travel a lot. Maybe she'd been too caught up in the aftermath of the bombing to answer her phone.

Or maybe she's dead.

No. No, she couldn't be. Not her. She was too good, too important to the welfare and safety of vampires and humans alike. If she was gone—especially at the hands of terrorists—there was going to be a *lot* more bloodshed.

Most of it human.

One thing was for sure, she was in no position at the moment to help us. Which meant we weren't going to Los Angeles.

"Well, we should call her. Larkin's apartment has a land-line," Kelly said, gesturing toward the phone sitting on a side table.

"I already did. A few minutes ago." I hated to even say the next words. "There was no answer."

"What do we do now?" Kelly sobbed.

Heather sounded equally as scared. "Where are we gonna *go*?"

I gave her the only viable answer left.

"Home."

15

LONG HAUL

The Bastion was the last place I wanted to go—but I didn't see any other choice. We needed help.

Vampire help.

"We can't go to our place in Los Angeles. The police will be watching it," Kelly said.

"I agree. I'm talking about Virginia. Now we need to find a vehicle to get us there. The Bastion's at least a three-day drive from here. There's no way we can ride on a bus with humans that long without being identified as vampires. We can't take Glenn's truck. The highway patrol will be looking for it soon if they're not already. We can't use a car service because the police will be notified if the driver's out of touch with their dispatcher for a long time."

"I thought Imogen said you could never come back if you left," Heather said.

A shudder went through me as I remembered my final farewell with my "mother." Imogen had been so angry at me for leaving, especially because I was leaving to go work for her sister.

"She did. But I don't see any other choice for us. She

won't turn you two away, at least. And it *is* a sanctuary. If we've ever needed one of those, it's now."

"Well, we're going to need a vehicle outfitted for daytime driving," Heather said.

"That'll be too suspicious. They'll know we're vampires. We'll be stopped and searched at every state line checkpoint."

"What will we do during the day then?" she asked. "We won't be able to stop and stay in hotels along the way without identification and money."

"Not to mention that would be a long haul without sleeping," Kelly said.

Long haul. My heart leapt with excitement. "I have an idea."

Going to the phone, I searched its speed dial directory. *Yes.* It was there—Curtis—the name of a vampire Larkin used to date.

The last time we'd spoken, she'd told me they had broken up but had agreed to be friends. I really hoped that was the case. I was about to ask Curtis for a very big favor.

I'd only spoken to him a handful of times, but he'd seemed like a super nice guy, respectful and generous and so clean-cut he looked like a choir boy. In fact, she'd met him at church.

Yes—vampires went to church. Not all of them of course, but of those who'd practiced a religion before turning, most I knew continued to observe their respective faiths.

Contrary to the opinions of some, vampirism had nothing to do with the occult or demons or even moral shortcomings. It was simply a biological condition, and in many cases, like mine, the vampire hadn't had a choice in the matter.

Speaking of prayer, I prayed Curtis hadn't disappeared

the way Larkin and Sadie had. His phone was ringing with no answer.

Maybe he was sleeping in. If so, I hated to wake him, but we really had no time to lose.

Finally, after about ten rings, he answered, sounding groggy. "Hello?"

"Curtis? Hi, it's Abigail."

"Abigail Byler? Where have you been? No one's heard from you in weeks. Larkin was frantic."

"Do you know where she is?" I asked, suddenly hopeful. Maybe they'd reconciled and Larkin was staying at his place.

"No. I mean, I assume she's either home or working at Fangers," he said.

"I don't think so. I'm at her place, and it's been abandoned. I can't reach Sadie either. Did you hear about what happened?"

"Yeah, I saw it on the news before I went to bed. Crazy, crazy stuff. I haven't talked to Larkin in at least a week. I hope she's okay. Are *you* okay, darlin'? It's not like you to go dark like that."

"I know. I'm sorry you were worried. Actually, I was arrested."

"Arrested? That's insane. You're Miss Straight and Narrow. For what?"

"I'm still not sure. Listen, I need help. I escaped with some friends of mine, and then a human died. It was self-defense, but the official reports are saying we murdered the guy and a bunch of others. I need to get to the Bastion."

"Oh Abbi, why would you go there? I thought you didn't believe in Imogen's approach."

"I don't. But we're in trouble, and Sadie is either dead, hurt, or in hiding. I don't know what else to do."

"How can I help?"

"Do you still have your big rig? Or did you sell it?"

"I've been trying to—Lord knows it's doing me no good sitting in my driveway, but I haven't been able to yet. Want to borrow it?"

"Could we rent it from you? I know you've had some money trouble since you got laid off."

Like so many vampires I knew, Curtis had lost his job. It happened a few months ago. He couldn't prove it was because he was a vampire, but no humans had been laid off from the trucking company that had employed him for the past twenty-five years—only the vampires.

It couldn't have been a case of age discrimination. His work record had been spotless. In fact, he'd been commended several times for his on-time deliveries and safe driving record.

"I can't pay you right now, but once we get to the Bastion I can send you some money," I said.

"I'm not gonna take your money, darlin'. You're a friend in need. I'd offer to drive you myself, but I've got some guests coming into town tomorrow."

"It's fine. I wouldn't want to put you at risk by association anyway. If we get caught in your truck, I'll say I stole it. They already think I'm a criminal. What's one more infraction?"

"Well, all right then. There's no trailer on it right now, so at least it'll be easier to park and handle. And it's got a curtained-off sleeping cab for daytime hours."

"I remember. Thank you so much, Curtis. You are literally a life saver."

"No problem. Happy to help. The thing I'm worried about is the state lines. Have you thought about that?"

All the major highways and most of the smaller ones had checkpoints at the state lines, part of a recent initiative to track the vampire population's travel patterns and ensure there were no mass gatherings of our kind, like conventions —or mobs.

Sadie's Devil's Night sit-in last year had caused an uproar with the human authorities.

"We're disguised as humans," I explained. "We've got colored contacts in."

"But they do temperature checks."

"Oh. Right."

Unescorted vampires weren't allowed to cross state lines without written work orders. We'd had no issues getting out to California from Virginia because we were coming to work for Sadie, and she'd pulled strings to make sure our papers were expedited.

But now... now we had a problem. Then it hit me...

We also have a human.

16

FRIENDS DON'T CUFF FRIENDS

Hopefulness zinged through my insides, giving me fresh energy in spite of my persistent thirst.

"I'll... work something out. Could you possibly bring the truck here?"

Curtis agreed, and I ended the call and filled my friends in on the plan.

"He'll be here in half an hour. It should be dark by then. I'm going to get changed. Take a look around for anything that might be useful on a road trip. We'll have to sort of rough-it camping in the truck during the daylight hours."

The only thing of Larkin's that fit me was a stretchy black tube skirt and a short top that exposed my whole stomach.

It was preferable to a prison uniform. Still, I winced at my reflection in the mirror. Since turning, I'd gradually given up the modest, extremely plain clothing I'd grown up wearing, but I was still miles away from an exhibitionist. This outfit was definitely not me. I was much more comfortable when people *weren't* noticing me.

After applying more makeup than I'd ever worn in my life, I chose a pair of blue contacts to cover my lilac irises.

My friends gave me a thumbs up when I joined them in the living room. "You look hot," Kelly teased, eyeing my out-of-character ensemble. "And human. Almost."

"And thirsty," Heather added before tossing me a full blood bag.

I caught it and stared down at the feast in my hands, my saliva spiking and my fangs jutting out instantly. I was starving. "Where did you get this?"

"From Larkin's freezer. That was the only one in there. I quick-thawed it in some hot water for you. It's gonna taste like garbage, but at least you won't die of thirst. You haven't had anything for days, except for that tiny little sip in the basement."

"You sure you don't want some?" My trembling fingers clenched greedily around the warm bag, contradicting my generous tone.

"No. You should have it. We already... had some," Kelly said in a chagrined way, obviously feeling guilty over drinking from Glenn.

"Okay, thanks." I drained the bag in mere minutes, grossed out at the less-than-fresh flavor but still hungry for more when it was gone.

Instantaneously I felt better, which was a good thing. We had a long drive ahead of us. It was better to be safe than sorry—especially when we would have human company for the trip.

Twisting the bathroom doorknob, I broke it off and pushed the door open. Shane jumped to his feet. He'd been sitting on the ledge of the garden tub.

His eyes scanned me from head to toe. "Wow. You... you came back."

"We never left. We ran into... complications—and *don't* say anything about the outfit."

"Your friend Sadie? Is she..."

"I don't know. I can't reach her. We're not going to Los Angeles anymore." I gritted my teeth then spat it out. "We're leaving the state... and you're coming with us."

Now he did a double-take for a different reason. "Me? Why?"

"A friend has an 18-wheeler we can borrow. It has a sheltered sleeping cab. But we can't travel over state lines without a human escort."

"Oh right. But I can't leave my uncle. He's sick."

"You'll have to. We need you. And he's a kidnapper. He was planning to starve us. He lied to you to get you to go along to the Safety Center and help with the breakout."

"I know, and I'm still mad at him over all of it. But he's my uncle, and he was desperate. He and my aunt gave me a place to live. I can't let him die alone—and that's a possibility."

"Where's your aunt now?"

"She lives in Davis, too, but they're separated."

"You'll just have to call her and ask her to look after him for a few days. Or she can hire a home health care nurse or something. You'll be gone three days at the most. When we get where we're going, I'll release you."

"Yeah, I've heard that one before. And then you locked me in a bathroom."

"I'm sorry. I'm telling you the truth though. You can drop us off and drive straight to an airport to fly home. We have no one else to ask."

"*Are* you asking?" Shane shot a wary look at the twisted blob of metal that used to be the doorknob. "Or are you telling?"

"Which one will get you into that truck?"

He let out a long breath. "Fine. But I have no idea how to drive a trailer truck."

Kelly stepped into the bedroom, obviously having overheard the conversation. "I do. I've got lots of truckers in my family. My uncles used to let me practice out on my granddad's land in West Virginia. It's not that hard once you get the hang of it."

"Okay, well, I guess I'll call my aunt while we wait for your friend to bring the truck," Shane said. "Wait—you killed my phone."

"There's a land line. You can use that."

I led him to the living room and took a seat on the sofa beside the phone, making it obvious I'd be listening in to ensure he didn't say anything about our current location or destination.

Shane shook his head. "Abigail... if I was going to turn you in, I would have done it already. I could have rear-ended a car on the way here, caused a fender bender and a traffic jam on the highway. I could have dialed 9-1-1 on my phone when you were in the back seat with a blanket draped over your head. I told you... I *want* to help you."

"Well... I guess now you'll have your chance."

ABOUT FORTY MINUTES LATER, Curtis called Larkin's apartment phone to let us know he was outside the building with the truck.

"I'm double parked so be quick about it," he said.

"We'll be right down," I assured him.

Apologizing once again, I placed the handcuffs around

Shane's wrists and locked them, pulling the sleeves of his jacket down to hide them as much as possible.

"You know you don't need these," he complained.

When we stepped out of the apartment building, a group of four men stood just outside the doors, smoking. They gave us appreciative glances. One let out a long wolf-whistle.

"Looks like the disguises work," Kelly said in a low, amused voice.

At the very least they kept the men from paying any notice to our human captive.

We ignored them and climbed into the rig's cab, where I exchanged hugs with Curtis. A teddy bear of a man, he had a ready smile and a deep laugh.

"Abigail. It's good to see you."

"You too. Thank you for coming. You're a literal lifesaver. These are my friends Heather and Kelly. And this is Shane," I said. "He's going to help us out with the border situation."

The older man looked from my face to Shane's and back again. "I see. So are you two—"

"No," I interrupted. "He's... a friend."

Shane rolled his eyes and lifted his arms, stretching them out to display his cuffed wrists. "Friends don't cuff friends."

It was true. We weren't friends. I'd coerced him into being there. It would be foolish to invest too much trust in him.

But he definitely didn't feel like an enemy either—not the way the prison guards had been. Or his uncles. Or those Coalition headquarters bombers, whoever they were.

"Okay then. Let's hope we don't get pulled over with a human passenger trussed up like a Thanksgiving turkey," Curtis said.

He put the truck in gear and navigated the city's tight, busy streets until we reached Highway 80 east. Just outside the city, he took an exit and parked in a truck stop lot.

"What's going on?" Heather asked. "Aren't we dropping you off at home?"

"Nope. Those alerts about you three are everywhere. It's best you get as far away from here as you can as quick as possible. Lisa can come pick me up—she's the woman I'm dating now. I'll just go in and have a drink till she gets here."

Extracting a wallet from his back pocket, he drew out some bills and offered them to me. "You'll need this for gas. This truck's served me well, but it has one hell of an appetite."

I looked longingly at the money. He was right. We did need it. But he was unemployed now. How could I take it from him?

I waved it away. "We can't take that. We'll figure something out."

"Like what? Putting those little outfits to use? Don't worry about it. I'll add this to your tab. You said you'd send me the money when you got to Virginia. I know you're good for it."

After I reluctantly accepted the cash, he turned to Shane. "And you—you take care of my girls. Anything happens to them, you'll have me to deal with, understand?"

"Got it, though..."

"Though what?" Curtis frowned in a way that made him look scary for the first time since, well maybe *ever*.

"Maybe you should be more worried about what's going to happen to *me*. I'm the one who's handcuffed and traveling cross country with three vampires."

Curtis held his gaze for a long moment then burst into laughter. "I like you, kid."

Wishing us luck, he hopped to the ground and strode toward the neon signs of the truck stop's restaurant, swinging one hand over his shoulder in a casual wave.

Kelly slid into the driver's seat. "Okay, let's see how far we can make it before daybreak. You two should crawl into the back and get some sleep. You were up all day long while we slept. I'll wake you both when we get to the first border checkpoint."

17

DANGEROUS

I t was a strange feeling to be on my way back to the Bastion. Honestly, I'd thought I'd never see it again.

The enormous cavern in Virginia's Shenandoah Valley served as the seat of the Crimson Court and the headquarters of the vampire resistance movement. That was only part of the reason I'd left.

No, my philosophical disagreements with Imogen hadn't been pleasant, but it was the constant temptation that had ultimately driven me away.

An image of Reece's dark-rimmed lilac eyes insinuated itself on my attempts to fall asleep. That and the discomfort of the colored contact lenses were making it an impossible task.

I stared up at the ceiling of the 18-wheeler's sleeping compartment, trying to keep still so at least Shane would be able to sleep.

"I thought silver was harmful to vampires," the quiet voice intruded on my thoughts.

Sitting up, I stared across the sleeping cabin at Shane. "What are you talking about?"

"Your necklace. It's silver, isn't it? You play with the pendant constantly. I thought it was supposed to burn you or something."

I looked down at the chain around my neck and the small silver dagger-like ornament hanging from it. Rubbing the red orb in the dagger's hilt, I answered him.

"Silver is fine. It's platinum that weakens us—that's what the cuffs are made of. It doesn't burn to the touch though."

"What about the pendant?"

"What about it?"

"Does it have any special significance? What is that red stone?"

"It's... not a stone. It's blood."

Shrugging, I let my pretended nonchalance cover a world of emotion as I was overcome by a hollow, hungry feeling that had nothing to do with my stomach.

For reasons I still couldn't understand, Reece had given me this necklace the night I'd left the Bastion. The blood inside the orb was his. "It's a vampire thing."

Shane nodded. "How'd you become one? A vampire? Did you choose it? Was it something you always wanted?"

It was an odd question, but I answered it. "No, I didn't choose it. I was in a highway accident, injured and near death. The vampire who turned me saved my life."

"Oh. Wow. I didn't think about it happening like that. What about your friends? How'd you meet?"

I glanced toward the privacy curtain that hung between us and them. The rumble of the road would obscure much of our conversation from their hearing, but I knew my friends wouldn't mind me telling him their stories anyway.

"We met at the place we're going now. It's sort of a... sanctuary, I guess, for vampires. Heather was already there when I got there. Her boyfriend, who was a vampire, abandoned her after turning her, so she was alone. Kelly got there about the same time I did. She was attacked by a group of nomadic rogue vampires. They left her for dead, and she woke up alone and really confused. She wandered around on the verge of starvation before she was found by the—"

I'd been about to say *Bloodbound* but stopped myself. Shane wasn't part of vampire society. He wouldn't understand Imogen's elite group of warriors even if I *was* allowed to tell him about them.

"...by some people from our group. We became friends there and then left together when we decided to work for Sadie Aldritch."

"Who do you think bombed the VHC headquarters?" he asked.

"They said on the news it was terrorists."

It had also occurred to me that human vampire haters were not the *only* enemies Sadie had. Would Imogen order a strike against her sister's organization?

It had been more than a year since I'd seen anyone from the Bastion. I assumed my vampire "mother" knew I'd gone to work for the VHC—and for her sister and ultimate rival. There wasn't much in the vampire world Imogen didn't know about.

Was it possible she'd been so angered by my defection she'd ordered the Bloodbound to bomb the building? Had she been trying to *kill* her sister?

And me?

I'd finally gotten the story behind their feud from Sadie one evening after work. It went all the way back to the Regency era when they'd both been turned as young women in England.

Like so many human rivalries, theirs had started with

a man.

"I hope Sadie's okay. She seems pretty cool," Shane said. "I've seen her on TV."

"You should meet her in person. She's beyond cool. She's a hero—our hero anyway. First, she drafted the Accord. Ever since then she's been a champion for vampire rights. She's tireless, and she's truly good."

"I'm not sure about her methodology though."

I nearly gasped at the insult. "What problem could you possibly have with her methodology? She's kept countless humans from being drained or turned. She's the strongest voice there is for peace between the species."

"That's just it. I think she might be *too* peaceful."

"There's no such thing. It's the only answer. Do you *want* a human-vampire war?"

"Of course not. I'm just saying while she talks about diplomacy and letting the courts and legislature handle things, President Parker keeps chipping away at vampire rights. I mean, they put you in what amounts to a prison camp for no reason. And according to my Uncle Glenn, they were planning to exterminate all of you—in all the camps. I'm not sure Sadie's message of non-violence isn't just letting him get away with it."

"You don't agree with the president's position?"

Shane rolled his eyes. "Do I *look* like I agree with him? Look where I am."

"Good point."

"I'm just saying I'm not sure peace at any cost is the way to go. It might benefit vampires to have a leader who's a little more... what's the word I'm looking for?"

"Scary?"

"Exactly. I mean, you're vampires. You're strong, you're fast, and if you wanted to be, you could be very dangerous. Maybe Parker would show more respect for vampires as a whole if your leader seemed more dangerous."

A picture of Imogen came to mind—a scene, actually. Her, sitting on her throne in the Grand Dome, ordering the public execution of a rogue vampire with a calm dip of her chin.

That vision was quickly followed by a memory of Imogen caressing Reece's neck and shoulders as he kneeled beside her throne, submitting to her authority as one of her personal guard.

How personal had things gotten between them since my departure?

Stop thinking about it. Just don't go there.

"You're only saying that because you've never actually met a dangerous vampire leader," I said.

"And you have?"

I stared at the vulnerable human, listening to his steady heartbeat and the sound of blood moving in his veins. Imogen would view him as nothing more than a food source. I shuddered to think of him—or any human—at her mercy.

"You should get some sleep."

There was no point in telling Shane about Imogen— he'd never meet her. We were going to have him drop us off in a town near the Bastion then he'd drive himself to the closest airport to fly home. We'd finish our journey on foot.

Not only did I not want Shane within twenty miles of that place, we weren't allowed to disclose its location to non-vampires for obvious reasons.

Of course when we got to Virginia and he dropped us

off, he'd have a rough idea of the region where the Bastion was located. But I doubted he'd ever suspect a cavern.

Even if he did, there were literally thousands of them in the state. More than four thousand to be exact, so the secret would remain safe.

I was determined Shane would, too.

18

MEN'S ROOM

I must have managed to fall asleep because I woke with a start when the rumble of the truck's engine cut abruptly.

Opening the heavy curtains between the cabins, I poked my head into the front seat. "Are we at another checkpoint?"

The one at the California-Nevada state line had been smooth sailing, but I was worried about the Utah one coming up.

"No. We're still in Nevada, at a truck stop," Kelly said. "This thing guzzles fuel. We need to fill it up."

"Okay. I'll wake Shane to see if he needs to use the bathroom or get some food or something."

When I withdrew into the sleeping cab again, his eyes were open.

"What's going on?" He yawned, blinking against the glare of bright gas station lighting coming through the gap in the curtains.

"We're refueling. Do you need anything? Food? Water? Restroom?"

Shane sat up and stretched his cuffed hands above his

head, giving another shuddering yawn.

"All of the above. So, what are we doing here, sheriff? Are you gonna parade me through the truck stop like a bounty hunter with her prey or can you take these off? It's not like they'd stop me from shouting for help if I planned to—which I don't. I've already told you I want to help you."

His face and the tone of his voice told me he meant what he was saying.

But it was a risk. If I took the cuffs off, he could make a run for it. If I left them on, it would certainly attract unwanted attention.

Besides, I wasn't sure as a guy he could even use the men's room with handcuffs on.

Withdrawing Glenn's keyring from my pocket, I gestured for Shane to extend his hands to me. I unlocked the cuffs with a stern warning. "I'm going in with you. I *am* a pacifist, but I assure you that won't stop me from doing whatever is necessary to protect my friends."

He rubbed one of his wrists then the other. "Yeah. I get it. It wasn't that long ago I watched you all kill my uncle."

Ouch. "That's right. And all it would take is a swipe of my hand to break your neck."

"Really Abigail. The tough act isn't necessary, and it doesn't suit you. Besides, if you were going to kill me, you'd have done it by now."

"Try to run or call for help, and you'll see exactly how well it suits me. I may not kill you, but I was trained in self-defense and hand to hand combat. I know lots of ways to hurt a person."

I half expected Shane to laugh at my threat—it sounded ridiculous to my own ears—but he simply nodded. We climbed out of the cab together, heading toward the truck stop's hospitality area.

Once inside, Shane went to the men's room while I waited just outside the door. Several other men entered during the next few minutes.

Only then did it occur to me—Shane could easily tell one of them he'd been kidnapped. He could ask them to call the police or to borrow their phone so he could do it.

Heart racing, I flung open the door and started inside. A hefty man in a worn Harley t-shirt and cowboy boots was coming out. He grinned widely.

"Well, hey there. Ladies' room is at the other end of the hall."

The grin turned lascivious as he got a good look at my outfit, the heavy makeup and clothes I'd borrowed from Larkin. "Or, if you want to come in here, I'll be happy to act as your personal escort."

For a moment I was frozen in indecision. My claims to Shane hadn't been false. I was quite capable of defending myself and could easily best this human man physically. But I didn't want to start any kind of altercation. It would draw attention to us, and if I did hurt the man and reveal my superior strength, out me as a vampire.

My face had been all over the news in California. Had it been here in Nevada as well? I had the colored contacts in, but if someone looked closely enough, they might recognize me as an escapee and "murderer."

"Oh. No. My mistake. Sorry." I tried backing out of the men's room, but the smiling man shot out a hand to grab my wrist and started dragging me inside.

"Stop. Let me go." My breathing accelerated, and I could feel my fangs emerging from my gums. I ducked my head to hide them and attempted to dig my heels into the painted concrete floor.

Just then Shane rounded the corner from the stall area.

I'd never been so happy to see his face. When he spotted me, his brows shot up before lowering over angry eyes.

He strode toward us and slid an arm around my back, settling his hand at my waist in a possessive gesture.

"What are you doing in here sweetheart? Is the ladies' room full?"

Sweetheart? Oh. It took me a minute to react, but I played along.

"Yes. The line is out the door," I lied. "And then I ran into this man when I was coming in."

The Harley guy, who'd released my wrist the instant he'd spotted Shane, held both hands up in the universal sign for surrender.

"Sorry man. I should have been watching where I was going." Darting his eyes to me, he mumbled, "Sorry," then turned and left the bathroom.

Shane's perturbed gaze followed him out the door then swung around to meet mine.

"Are you okay? What happened?"

One of the men who'd entered the bathroom after Shane rounded the corner from the stalls and went to a sink. He snuck repeated glances at us while he washed his hands.

Aware of him, I avoided Shane's question. "I'm fine. Everything's fine."

Noticing the man as well, Shane nodded in understanding. "Go on back to the truck. I'm going to wash up and grab some bottled water and snacks, and I'll meet you out there in a minute."

"I'd rather wait for you," I said. But the hand-washing man was now looking directly at me.

Did he recognize me? Maybe it was just the skimpy

outfit. He probably thought I was one of those women who hung around truck stops looking for "customers."

I had a decision to make—follow Shane's suggestion and take the chance he'd ask someone inside the truck stop for help—or stay here to watch him while this guy and who knew who else watched *me.*

"I'll see you outside," I said and left the bathroom.

Back at the truck, Heather was returning the gas nozzle to its hook. She was clearly surprised to see me returning alone.

"Where's Shane?"

"He's getting some food and drinks. He'll be out in a minute." I paused then added, "I hope."

"You trust him that much?" she asked.

"Not really but I didn't have much choice. A man was staring at me in there."

She sucked in a breath. "Did he recognize you?"

"I'm not sure. It might have been because I look like a prostitute. Or maybe it was because I was in the men's room."

"What?" she asked, laughing and looking far more relaxed now.

Before I could explain, she said, "Oh, here he comes."

I whirled around, halfway expecting to see Shane accompanied by a highway patrol officer or at least a couple of burly truckers, but he was alone.

Without a word, he opened the cab's back door and got inside.

I looked at Heather.

"Okay then," she said.

"Okay then. Let's get back on the road and get out of here just in case that guy did recognize me."

19

SPOONING

The fresh tank of gas would have lasted beyond dawn, but of course we had to get off the road before the sun came up.

We'd made good time, which in some ways was good, but bad in another way. We had made it through Utah and into Wyoming, which had a policy allowing individual businesses to choose whether they wanted to serve vampires or not.

The first few hotels we stopped at had signs reading "No Vampires" prominently displayed in their front windows.

"I don't think we can make it to the next exit before sunrise," Kelly said, sounding worried.

"There's a rest stop in two miles," I said. "We'll park there and sleep in the back."

I had moved to the front seat to keep Kelly company for a while, and Heather now rode in the back with Shane. As it was still dark, the curtain between the two areas was open.

Shane was obviously awake and had heard us because he responded.

"You know, if Kelly gave me a few pointers, I could drive

102

during the daylight hours while you three sleep back here. We'd get there in half the time."

"No."

I didn't have to even consider my answer. The thought of the three of us unconscious and vulnerable while he drove us anywhere he wanted sent shivers down my spine.

"We'll all stay in the back together. We can get underway again at darkfall."

Shane gave me a disappointed look. "I would think you'd trust me after the truck stop."

A twinge of guilt tweaked my chest. "I'm sorry, but the past few weeks have shaken my trust in humanity a bit."

"I'm not 'humanity,'" he said. "I'm me. There's a difference."

"Not from where I sit," Heather said sleepily.

Then her tone turned teasing. "What's the matter? Don't want to spoon with three hot vampire chicks? There are a lot of men who'd kill to be in that position—or die to."

I couldn't help it. I laughed at her terribly inappropriate joke, but Shane didn't. In fact, he appeared to be sulking.

Sobering, I said, "We just can't afford to take any chances, okay? We have to get where we're going. I have to protect my friends."

"I could be your friend," he said, "if you'd let me."

We parked at the rest area, and Shane used the restroom before we locked ourselves back inside the big rig and closed the light-blocking curtains, sealing the Velcro strips that held them together.

The conditions were a bit cramped. Still, we were safe. Curtis's truck had been the perfect choice of vehicle for interstate travel.

My friends and I decided to take shifts, two of us sleeping while one stood guard over the truck and our human passenger. Because I'd slept some during the night hours, I took the first watch.

Shane, who'd also slept most of the night, was wakeful now.

"Do you really think I'd turn you in?" he asked quietly.

I studied his face in the dim gray atmosphere of the sleeping cabin.

"No. Not really," I admitted. "But there *is* always a chance. Contrary to some reports, vampires can't read minds. And apparently, a lot of people hate us."

"I don't hate vampires." There was a long pause. "I loved one once actually."

"What? You had a vampire girlfriend?"

"I did. We worked together at a movie theater when I was in high school. Her name was Marjorie," he said.

"I remember you said you were in love once. Why did you break up?"

His fond expression soured. "My parents forced me to end things with her."

"Oh. They didn't like vampires?"

"They didn't know anything about them at the time," he explained. "But then they saw some bite marks on me. They freaked out. I told them I had no intention of turning, that I was perfectly safe with Marjorie and really happy, but their minds were made up. They basically threatened to kick me out if I didn't stop seeing her."

He lifted his shoulders and let them fall. "So I did."

"I'm sorry," I said, and I was. It wasn't so long ago I'd been under the complete control of my parents. I also understood how hard it was to give up someone you loved because your hand was forced.

"Maybe it's not too late for you two. Did you ever look her up after they... you know... died?"

At least I assumed his parents were dead. He'd hinted at it and told me he'd gone to live with his aunt and uncle.

Shane shook his head. "I did, but she'd moved on. She had a serious boyfriend. A vampire. I decided not to rock the boat, to let her be happy. He was probably better for her anyway."

The look in his eyes turned speculative. "Have you ever been in love? Or wait—do you have a mate?"

Blushing for no good reason, I said, "I don't. I don't even really date. There was a guy once. It didn't work out." *To say the least.*

"Well maybe it's not too late for *you*. I mean if he still lives in this place we're going..."

"No, it's over. For good. He's made an eternal commitment to..." I'd almost slipped and said Imogen's name. "...someone else."

Shane nodded thoughtfully. "Well, when you're ready to move on, you'll have no shortage of opportunity I'm sure. You're a beautiful girl. Any guy—vampire or human— would be lucky to have you."

A tingly sense of pleasure mixed with hot embarrassment. For one thing, I wasn't used to receiving compliments. For another, he was completely wrong.

"Thank you. I'd never date a human though."

His brow creased. "I didn't peg you for a human hater."

"No. Not at all. I'm not. It's just... not safe."

How could I explain to him the temptation produced by the smell of his blood? Or the terror I felt whenever I thought about the possibility of inadvertently hurting someone I loved? It had kept me away from my birth family and humans in general.

One slip-up could mean death for them. And what had happened to Josiah and his family was always with me.

I couldn't risk it happening again to another guy I cared for or called a friend.

Suddenly hyper-aware of his heartbeat, I scooted farther from Shane.

He must have sensed my discomfort because he said, "It's okay, you don't owe me any explanations. I mean, in a couple of days, we'll never see each other again, right?"

I nodded, speaking quietly. "Right. You can drop us off and get back to your life."

"Yes. My wonderful life," he quipped.

"I'm sorry about all this," I said. "Forcing you to come with us, the handcuffs."

"Yeah, I could have lived without those for sure. They rubbed my wrists raw."

He held his arms out to me, and I looked down at his wrists. Sure enough, the flesh there was reddened and abraded. A couple of spots were even bleeding.

Oh God.

Fierce thirst hit my throat like wildfire. The truck stop hadn't sold blood bags, and I'd had nothing to drink since that defrosted blood bag at Larkin's apartment yesterday.

My fangs did their irritating involuntary response thing, sliding from my gums and pushing past my lips. My stomach growled loudly.

Instead of cowering in fear or looking horrified, Shane actually laughed. "Oh, sorry. I guess I shouldn't have dangled chum in front of the shark. You must be thirsty."

I nodded. "It's okay. I am, but you're not in danger. I got used to being thirsty in the Safety Center. Feedings were once daily, and the rations were small. I can go for a while without blood when I have to."

He glanced over at my sleeping friends. "What about them?"

"I'm sure they're thirsty too. Maybe when we get to Nebraska we'll start seeing some signs along the highway for vampire-friendly exits. We can get off at one and buy some blood bags."

"Yeah, I think I saw a billboard a little while ago about a place that had them at one of the next few exits," he said.

"Good. That's perfect." I yawned loudly.

He chuckled. "Am I boring you?"

"No. I'm sorry. It's really hard for us to stay awake when the sun is up. We can do it in an emergency, but when there's no threat or reason to stay awake, it's tough."

"No, I understand. I remember Marjorie being like that. I was just kidding. You can go ahead and sleep you know. I'm not going to try to bolt."

"I know that. I do need to wake one of them to take a shift though before I doze off. Not for my sake—I believe you—but it'll make them feel safer."

"Sure," he said, sounding displeased despite his words of agreement. "I understand."

I woke Heather for her shift then slumped into a dreamless sleep, resting deeply in spite of the crowded conditions in the truck's rear cabin.

My incarceration had also taught me to sleep in uncomfortable circumstances. Our cots at the Safety Center had been narrow and hard with a thin blanket and no pillow.

When I awoke sometime later, I blinked a few times and looked around in confusion.

Where am I?

The Safety Center was so much warmer than usual.

Oh, it wasn't the Safety Center. I was in the truck. We were on our way to the Bastion.

Butterflies swam in my belly at the mere thought of the place. Of *him*. I clutched my ever-present pendant, feeling the familiar contours of the tiny dagger and the smooth roundness of the orb in its hilt.

What would Reece do when we arrived? What would he say? Would Imogen decide to get theatrical and send him personally to carry out the death sentence she'd threatened me with if I ever returned?

Perhaps she already knew I was on my way home. I'd been told that as my maker she could always sense my location.

That knowledge had given me many moments of fear over the past months—anytime I was alone at home or walking somewhere in the city.

She could have sent Kannon or any of the other Blood-bound after me to grab me off the street and forcibly return me to the Crimson Court. But she never had.

And contrary to Heather and Kelly's hopes, she hadn't sent anyone to rescue us when we'd been arrested and held in the Safety Center.

As far as I could tell, my "mother" had washed her beautiful, terrifying hands of me. If we'd had any choice whatsoever, we wouldn't be putting ourselves at the mercy of them again.

Speaking of hands, I hoped Shane's were beginning to heal and he'd rested more comfortably without the cuffs on this time. In the dim light, I couldn't separate his shadowed form from that of my friends.

"Heather," I whispered to keep from waking him and Kelly.

No answer. Had she dozed off too?

"Heather," I said more loudly, and this time a drowsy, "Hmmm?" sound came in response.

"Did you fall asleep?"

"No," she said, sounding confused. "Oh, wait. I think so. I'm sorry. Everything was so quiet and cozy back here."

"It's okay. I wonder what time it is?"

Moving carefully so as not to jostle our still-sleeping companions, I parted the curtain slightly to peek through the windshield and check the position of the sun. A pinkish-purple glow lit the sky.

"It's almost sunset. We should wake them and get ready to go."

I could hear Heather move, slowly at first and then a rapid, panicky sounding motion. She sat straight up.

"Where's Shane?"

20

SLOW NIGHT

"What do you mean?" I demanded, trying hard to keep my pulse steady.

"He's not here," Heather said. "He's gone."

"That's impossible. We would have heard him get out. The sun would have burned us when he opened the door."

"Not if he hung a blanket over the doorway," she said, ripping down a blanket that had been hung over one of the doors.

So much for the steady pulse. Mine skyrocketed, and a whirring noise filled my ears. I couldn't believe it.

After our "heartfelt" discussion this morning and all his declarations of wanting to help, Shane had ditched us.

Maybe I'd scared him off by talking about how thirsty we all were.

"How'd he even manage to do all that with the cuffs on?" Heather asked.

Wincing in shame, I lifted the restraining device with the edge of a blanket and held it up for her.

"I left them off. Because I decided to trust him. Like an idiot."

"I can hardly point fingers," she said. "I fell asleep on my watch. I just can't believe we didn't wake up when he got out."

"We're all low on blood," I said. "Our senses are dulled, and it makes the exhaustion worse."

"You can say that again. Maybe it's a good thing for the human that he *did* leave. I have to admit he was starting to look pretty tasty last night. He smells good too."

"Yeah, he does," I admitted. "Wake up Kelly. It'll be dark any minute now. We need to get going as soon as possible in case Shane decided to report us."

I feared it might already be too late. When the sun went down and we climbed into the front cab, there very well might be a squad of police cars surrounding the truck.

Just then the back door opened. Heather cringed back instinctively to avoid the light, but there was none. It was dusk.

Shane stood outside the truck, smiling up at us.

"Good evening, ladies."

He came back.

I could hardly believe it. Why? Why hadn't he run? Had he just gotten out to go to the bathroom? That possibility had never occurred to me when I'd learned he was missing. I was sure we'd seen the last of him.

Shane climbed into the back of the truck and shut the door behind him. Now that I was no longer in shock, I noticed he held a plastic shopping bag.

Reaching inside it, he withdrew a blood bag and then another and another. "Breakfast is served."

My jaw dropped open, and not because I was about to bite him. "You went out to... buy blood?"

He chuckled. "I couldn't sleep. You three were out cold, and I figured I could use a stretch of the legs, so I walked to the next exit—the one I saw on that billboard, remember? The truck stop there had a refrigerated case of blood bags. I figured it would save us time today—and also save my neck —if I got some 'supplies' for you."

Heather grabbed at one of the bags with greedy hands, and Kelly, who'd awakened at hearing all the chatter, did the same. I took the third one from him more slowly, nearly catatonic with disbelief. And relief.

"Thank you," I whispered.

He chuckled again. "Tell the truth. You thought I ran off, didn't you?"

"Honestly? Yes. Why didn't you?"

"*Why* is it so hard to believe I legitimately want to help you?"

"Because it *is*," I said. "I mean, we didn't exactly get off to a great start, and I had you in handcuffs—until yesterday. You must have some ulterior motive for staying with us."

Shane's expression froze for a second. I'd offended him. It wasn't like he was some sort of double agent trying to discover the location of the vampire resistance stronghold.

I was about to apologize when his usual sense of calm returned. "I guess I can't blame you if your time in the Safety Center made you suspicious of humans. My Uncle Glenn was part of the reason, and I'm sorry for that. You know I feel bad about what he and Terry did to you, and I told you about my past connection to Marjorie. Just call me... an ally."

I studied his face, looking for signs of duplicity. There were none. Just Shane's sweet brown eyes looking back at me.

Suddenly I felt silly for thinking the worst of him. Even more than that, I was profoundly grateful to have something to drink. "Thank you for coming back. And for the blood bags."

"You're welcome. So... we should get going, huh?"

I nodded. "Yes. I think you should ride up front with Kelly for a bit since we're close to the Nebraska state border."

Later tonight, we'd cross through Iowa and Illinois as well. The first few state line checkpoints had been no problem. The agents on duty had given the truck—and Kelly and Shane—bored once overs before waving them through. But during our training at the Bastion, our survival instructor Eudora had told us the checkpoints got more and more rigorous the farther east you went.

The two of them climbed into the front cab, and we set off.

Leaving the curtain between the compartments open, I watched the miles pass through the windshield. It was a calm night weather-wise, and the highway traffic was sparse.

It was an hour before dawn when we reached the Pennsylvania state line. Seeing the state welcome sign pinged my heart with an unexpected sense of nostalgia.

"Hey—Pennsylvania. Isn't that where you're from?" Heather asked.

I gave her a terse nod and didn't elaborate. Instead, I asked Kelly, "Remember your lines?"

We all wore our colored contacts in the hopes of preventing temperature checks, but we'd rehearsed an explanation in case of one.

"Of course. But I won't need them," she said. "These guys don't even care."

"Don't get cocky," I warned.

Heather and I stayed in the back out of sight. I fastened the privacy curtain, leaving a tiny gap to peek through. I'd be able to hear every word, but I wanted to keep an eye on the situation as well.

The truck slowed as it approached the squat, brightly lit government building. A door on its side opened, and a uniformed agent stepped out. He was middle-aged with thinning blond and gray hair cut very short. He looked sleepy, as if we might have caught him dozing.

Kelly lowered the driver's side window, offering the agent a cheery greeting.

"Hi. Slow night?"

He gave her a guilty grin. "Little bit, but this time of night is always slow. Making good time?"

"It's been great. I'm so glad it's not raining."

The agent nodded to Shane. "Evening."

"How's it going?" Shane said then joked, "I'm glad it's not raining too. She's a hell of a driver, but when the rain kicks in she's ready to get off the road and find a hotel."

"Hey—you're making me sound like a wimp." She gave Shane's arm a playful slap.

The guard chuckled but didn't wave them through or raise the barrier arm in front of the truck.

"May I see your registration?"

"Sure." Kelly kept her tone calm, but when she turned away from him toward Shane, her eyes were wide with panic. "Would you get that out of the glove box, sweetie?"

Shane opened it and dug around, finally producing the document. Kelly passed it to the agent who studied it with a frown.

"This says the truck is registered to a Curtis Gaynor. Says he's a vampire."

To her credit, Kelly stayed cool. She told the story we'd agreed upon at the beginning of our trip. "Yes. He's my uncle. He's retired and selling his truck to a human driver.

He doesn't have an interstate travel pass anymore, so Uncle Curtis asked me to deliver it to the buyer."

The agent's eyes narrowed. Did he doubt her story? "I see. And where is this buyer?"

"New York. My uncle really needs the money now that he's not working. And the buyer really needs it so he can start driving."

The agent seemed somewhat assuaged. He nodded, and his tone turned snarky. "Well, it's good to see some humans getting back to work now that the vamps aren't taking all the jobs."

As far as I could tell, Kelly didn't flinch. Neither did Shane. In fact, he nodded along with the man's statement, pretending to agree. At least I assumed he was pretending.

The agent handed the registration back to Kelly, and her shoulders relaxed.

"Thanks. Have a good night," she said.

"One more thing." Reaching for his utility belt, the agent drew out a temperature wand.

Oh no.

"We're supposed to do random checks, and I'm low on my quota. Like I said, slow night."

21

TRUE NATURE

I worked to calm my nerves.

It's going to be okay. This was why we'd brought Shane along in the first place.

It was legal for a vampire to cross state lines—with a human or a special pass. But Kelly wasn't just any vampire. She was wanted by the federal authorities, like the rest of us.

My hope had been that she'd pass for human and be waved through with no questions. My new hope was that the agent wouldn't see through her disguise.

"No problem." Kelly leaned toward the open window, giving the man easy access to her forehead with the wand.

The device beeped, and the guard squinted at the digital readout, looking unhappy. "Running a little cool there."

"My boyfriend likes to ride with the windows down," she said brightly. "Even when it's cold out. Good thing he's so cute."

She smiled over at Shane, who played along. "I get carsick," he said with a sheepish grin. "*Of course* I'd go and fall in love with a truck driver."

The agent looked at the temperature device again, biting

the inside of one cheek. Was this it? Was this where we got busted? The agent walked around to the passenger side, and Shane took his turn with the temp wand.

"Is it just you two?" the agent asked him. "No passengers?"

"Nope, just us," Shane lied.

Panicked, I drew back from the curtains. Heather, who was able to hear the conversation as clearly as I was, growled quietly beside me.

"We might have to take him out," she whispered.

"We're not taking *anyone* out. It's going to be fine." Inside, I admitted she might be right. This might lead to an altercation.

"Sir, can I ask you to get out of the truck for a minute?" the agent asked Shane.

Oh, this wasn't good. At *all*.

I could tell from the sound of the passenger door opening Shane had complied. Once the door shut again, the agent lowered his voice to a whisper—as if a vampire couldn't hear that through a steel door—and spoke to Shane in a serious tone.

"Son... I'm not sure you realize it, but you're traveling with a vampire."

No response from Shane. The agent went on.

"Now that's not illegal, and you're welcome to do whatever floats your boat. I just wanted to make sure you're aware of it."

Finally Shane answered. "Yes sir, I realize that. That doesn't bother me. But thank you for looking out."

"Okay well, she's wearing colored contact lenses. I thought she might be attempting to hide her true nature from you."

The agent sounded almost disappointed. Maybe he was bored and hoping for some action?

"And I wanted to make sure you're with her voluntarily—not under any sort of duress," he said.

"No, sir. Nothing like that. I want to be with her. She's my girlfriend. She thinks I don't know, but I do. We just haven't had 'the talk' yet. But I'm fine."

Shane was doing an amazing acting job. He added, "She's a really nice girl."

"Yeah, well... you're young," the agent said. "You haven't seen as much as I have, but like I said, you're an adult. You can do what you like. I'd just... just watch your back, okay?"

"Yes sir, I will. Thank you."

The passenger door opened and closed again. Seconds later, the truck rolled forward. *Thank God.*

As soon as we were away from the lights of the checkpoint, I ripped open the curtains.

"What do you think?" I asked Kelly and Shane.

They didn't have to ask for clarification. They understood I was asking whether they thought the agent had reported a suspicious vampire.

"He radioed someone the minute we pulled away." Kelly's face was pinched with worry. "I saw him in the mirror."

"I didn't like the look in his eyes. I think we should ditch the truck," Shane said in a grim tone.

I nodded. "That's what I'm thinking too. There was something in his voice. I'm betting he flagged us."

Glancing in the side view mirror again, I searched the dark highway behind us for colored flashing lights.

"If we ditch the truck, how will we get there?" Heather asked. "Are we close enough to travel on foot?"

I looked out the window at a passing mile marker,

knowing exactly where we were. "We *could*. I don't know—it's risky."

We were still about three hundred miles away. We'd let Shane go on his way of course, but with all the police alerts out, three female vampires traveling on foot would raise suspicions.

"I can't guarantee we'd be able to find good cover the whole way," I told her. "And there's the issue of daylight. We'd have to find somewhere safe to sleep. Fast."

"Maybe we can steal a UV-treated car?" Shane suggested.

"There would be a theft report," I said. "And we'd only be trading one wanted vehicle for another—not to mention the fact UV-treated cars get extra attention at checkpoints. Besides, if they *do* end up catching us before we can make it home, I don't want them to have any legitimate charges against us."

My mind turned it over as I watched the blackness of night begin to lift. "I've been trying to think about how Sadie would handle this whole thing. She'd say to 'stay on the right side,' not to lower ourselves to the level of those who persecute us. I'm sure when we're able to contact her, the VHC will help us get good lawyers who can prove we had nothing to do with the break-in at the Safety Center and that you killed Glenn in self-defense."

"Yeah, if the VHC still *exists*," Heather said, sounding glum. "And if Sadie's still alive."

"She *is*," I insisted. She *had* to be. Not only were we screwed without her, the whole world was. "Right now, we just need to focus on getting to safety."

"And find a place to spend the day where we won't get toasted," Kelly added.

"I have an idea," I said. "Take this next exit."

"Where are we going?" She put on the right turn signal and switched lanes.

"I know of a place we can hide the truck—and find an inconspicuous vehicle."

22

___

SCENE OF THE CRIME

The glow of impending dawn colored the horizon as we pulled into the village where I'd grown up.

Eying the lightening sky, Kelly tightened her grip on the steering wheel. "Are we almost there?"

"It's your next left," I assured her. "We're very close."

A few men were already out in the fields—the day started early for Amish people—but I didn't worry about them giving our truck any special notice. There were truck drivers who lived in our rural area. The farmers would assume this rig belonged to one of them.

Amish people tended to mind their own business anyway and not concern themselves overmuch with the affairs of "the English" outsiders.

I only hoped the barn where I planned to hide the truck still stood empty and unused.

As the members of my old community all had their own homes and farms, I doubted anyone would have moved into this one—especially after the ghastly thing that had happened there.

Sure enough, when we turned onto the long drive

leading to the Yoders' house and barn, there were no lights to be seen, no activity at all.

"What is this place?" Kelly whispered, though of course no one could hear her.

"It's the home of an old friend. It's... unoccupied. This is the village where I grew up."

"Oh wow. I've never been in an Amish house before," Heather said.

"You won't be in one tonight either," I said. "We're going to sleep in the barn. We can pull the truck in through the barn doors and hide it in there. You all can sleep in the back. I'm going to sleep up in the hay loft and keep an ear out in case anyone comes down the drive."

Shane craned his neck toward the dark house. "Darn it. I was kind of hoping for a real bed tonight—and a little more space—no offense, ladies. Any reason we can't sleep in the house? You said it's unoccupied. What, you think the owners will be mad?"

"The owners are dead," I said and left it at that.

He didn't ask any more questions, just stayed quiet until we pulled up to the barn doors. He and I got out and hurriedly opened them, and Kelly drove the big rig inside.

Only after we rolled the doors closed behind it, did I breathe a sigh of relief.

We were safe, and not a moment too soon. The slats between the boards of the barn walls turned bright orange as the sun crested the horizon.

Heather opened the truck's back door and poked out her head, looking around. "That was tight. Thank God you thought of this place." She yawned loudly. "I'm exhausted. See y'all tonight."

Then she backed into the cab again, disappearing into the dark cocoon where we'd spent the past couple of days.

Kelly rolled down the truck's driver's side window. She looked beat as well. "You want me to take first watch, or..."

"No. Don't worry about it," I said. "You did your part by driving all night long. Thanks by the way—you did great."

"Thanks." She disappeared from view, climbing into the back with Heather to sleep.

Shane looked at me, lifting his brows. "So... I guess you're on first watch again?"

I shook my head. "For the police or curious locals—not for you. I know that isn't necessary. You more than proved yourself last night with the blood bags and the whole 'my girlfriend' story at that last checkpoint. You were very convincing by the way."

He laughed. "High school theater. I thank you, and Mrs. Dunn, the drama program sponsor, thanks you."

I started climbing the ladder. Instead of getting into the truck cab, Shane followed me. "What are you doing?" I asked over my shoulder.

"Figured you could use some company. Besides, I wasn't kidding about the space issue in that sleeping cab. I couldn't stretch out my legs all the way, and I got a wicked kink in my back. And... there are a *few* things humans can do that you can't."

"What do you mean?"

When we reached the top of the ladder, he demonstrated his point by going to the loft's opening and closing the old plywood door to block out the morning light.

"Ta da."

I smiled. "Thank you. I might have gotten a rude awakening as the day went on and the sun shifted positions."

"You're already hot enough," he quipped. "No need for flames."

He meant it as a joke—or a compliment—but the

remark caused a stab of pain in my abdomen. On this very property was the spot where Josiah had stood and allowed the sun to end his brand-new vampire life.

Being here made me feel sort of like a criminal returning to the scene of the crime.

I settled onto the floor near the front of the loft where I could peek out and quickly identify any threats, to rouse my friends should I hear someone pull into the driveway or enter the barn.

Shane leaned back against a nearby hay bale and stretched out his legs, crossing them at the ankles. Plucking a straw from the floorboards, he twirled it between his fingers, but his eyes were on me. It made me uncomfortable.

"Your wrists look better," I said for something to say. His skin there was still pink but no longer raw.

"They feel better." He checked himself, holding up one hand then the other and twisting them in front of his face. "I'm glad you trust me enough now to skip the cuffs. It would do me zero good to try to run away anyway. I have no freaking idea where I am."

"We're not that far from civilization. It only feels that way."

"You grew up here?" he asked.

"Right next door. Of course, 'right next door' is a couple miles away. Welcome to the sticks of Pennsylvania."

"So then... is this where we were heading all this time? Your home?" He seemed a little disappointed.

"It isn't my home anymore. Hasn't been for a while... since I turned. But we're not too far away. Our destination is only about five hours from here."

"Have to say, I never would have guessed you were Amish."

"There are a lot of things you don't know about me." *And a lot of things you'll never know.*

"Like what?"

For a moment I just looked at him, this human guy who'd come into my life so suddenly and strangely. Our shared journey was almost at an end.

Tonight, we'd go our separate ways, and I'd never see him again. Never talk to him again. It was weird to think of a person playing such a pivotal role in your life—literally *saving* your life—and then—*poof*—they're gone like they never existed.

There really was no point in a tell-me-your-life-story chat. Still, I answered him.

"Well, I can milk a cow. I can sew. I can make homemade butter, and I bake bread like nobody's business."

Placing a hand over his heart, he dramatically stretched the other arm toward me. "Marry me."

He was joking, but I wasn't laughing. He'd inadvertently hit on a sore spot.

According to Imogen I'd never be able to marry—not if I accepted my "destiny" in the vampire world anyway.

And suddenly I was overcome with irritation. Why were Shane and I sitting up talking instead of getting some sleep? We weren't on a date. We weren't even friends, not really. I wasn't sure why he'd even be interested in knowing anything about me.

"I'll never get married," I said more harshly than I probably should have. "I'll never have babies."

"I'm sorry." He paused, looking hesitant to ask, but he did it anyway. "Did you want to, you know, before?"

"One day, when the time was right. I always assumed I'd be a mother someday."

"You would have made a great one." He played with the

straw in his fingers, pulling it apart. "It seems like the marriage thing is still on the table, though. I mean, I've met married vampires before. And plenty of human men don't care about the baby thing and would love to be with you, too."

His eyes left the tattered piece of straw and came up to meet mine. "Take my word for it."

I glared at him. "If that's true then they're stupid. It's completely out of the question. It's too dangerous to be with a human. One wrong move, and I could kill him."

Using as intimidating a tone as I could muster, I added, "Never forget that. Your girlfriend Marjorie... Kelly, Heather... me... every vampire you've ever met—we're dangerous predators."

Shane's gaze locked on me, and his heartbeat, which I could hear clearly, increased in pace.

"I'm not scared of you, you know." His tone wasn't quite seductive, but it was definitely *something*.

Wait... *no*. It couldn't be. We'd *kidnapped* him for God's sake. Was this why he'd stayed with us when he could have escaped? Did he *feel* something for me?

Did the pheromone thing affect human males as well as vampires?

If that was the case, I had to shut this down right now.

"You should be," I said, staring into his intense brown eyes. "I'm a murderer."

23

A RATHER SIGNIFICANT DETAIL

For long moments, Shane stayed quiet and still. I'd shocked him.

Good. He needed to understand what he was dealing with. There *were* lots of good vampires in the world, but there were plenty of bad ones too.

We were headed right for a hotbed of them.

His experience with Marjorie had probably led him to believe all vampires were like her.

"You couldn't be a murderer," he finally said. "I don't believe it."

"Someone is dead because of me. Several people, actually."

"Who?"

I peered through a knothole at the Yoders' lifeless house, at Josiah's vacant bedroom window. "My friend Josiah, the boy who lived here. We'd been friends since we were two. He liked me."

"Of course he did," Shane said, but I ignored his ignorant compliment and kept going.

"We were in an accident on the highway. All of us should

probably have died on the scene, but a group of vampires was passing through and found us. One of them turned me."

I took a deep breath before continuing, remembering that night. "I turned Josiah the next day. I bit him, drank his blood. One of my best friends. I *drank* his *blood.* He was the first and last person I ever bit."

"You were a brand-new vampire," Shane argued. "Marjorie told me what that was like. I'm sure you didn't mean to."

"I did. That's the thing. I thought about it beforehand, and I chose to do that to him. I told myself I was saving his life, but the end result was still the same. A few days later he came home and slaughtered his parents then took his own life. A whole family wiped out. All their blood is on my hands. Even if I really do live for eternity, I'll never live that down. I'll never stop seeing that look in Josiah's eyes when he told me I should have just let him die in the hospital. He was right."

"You made a mistake. You've gotta stop torturing yourself, Abigail."

I turned to Shane, angry though I wasn't exactly sure why.

"Really?" I demanded. "Why? I think it's only fitting that I torture myself. It's no less than I deserve."

Wow—I sound just like Reece.

It was impossible not to think of him in this place. He'd been there that first night of my vampire life. He blamed himself as well.

Now it was Shane's turn to get angry. His face reddened, and his voice dropped into a lower register.

"Do you think you're the only person in the world with regrets? The only person who screwed up and can never take it back? I *did* want to help you, like I said, but you were right—there *is* another reason I came with you willingly, Abigail... a reason I didn't escape when I had the chance."

I blinked. Blinked again. Shane had shocked me. *Did* he actually have some ulterior motive all along?

"What is it?"

"When I told you about my parents earlier, about how they didn't approve of me and Marjorie, I left out a rather significant detail." He took a deep breath and let it out. "They're vampires."

Crackling electricity zapped all my senses. "*What*?"

"My parents are vampires. They weren't at the time I was seeing Marjorie, when they forced me to break up with her and told me how "evil" she and the rest of the vampire race were. A couple of years later they were both turned—involuntarily. Suddenly they saw vampires a little differently. Suddenly they were asking for understanding and compassion."

He frowned at the memory of some long-ago conversation. "I didn't give it to them."

"You were angry at their sudden change of heart," I said, getting it completely.

He nodded. "All I could think at the time was what hypocrites they were. They'd forced me to break up with a girl I loved for reasons beyond her control. It was different when it affected *them*, though. After they turned, they begged my forgiveness, but I didn't want anything to do with them. I decided to go live with my uncle and aunt. They gladly took me in. They disapproved of my parents' new lifestyle and didn't think it was healthy for a human kid to live with a couple of vampires. I didn't even speak to my parents for a long time. Finally, last Christmas, I called them. I realized I'd been pretty immature about the whole thing. I missed them, and I'd been thinking about it a lot, deciding maybe I'd made a mistake, cutting them off like that."

"What happened? What did they say?"

He shook his head. "Their phone was disconnected. I drove by the house and saw it had been sold. My uncle never even mentioned to me they were planning to move. I haven't spoken to them in a couple of years now. I have no idea where they are or how to find them. They didn't leave a forwarding address or tell anyone where they were going."

My first thought—a frightening one—was that they'd been taken to a Safety Center like my friends and I had been, like many of our neighbors had been.

Hopefully that wasn't the case. Perhaps Shane's parents really had simply elected to move away and start fresh somewhere new. Being here in this barn underlined for me how old memories could haunt a place.

"You thought we might be able to help you find them," I said rather than asked.

He nodded his confirmation. "I figured if you're going to a 'safe place' as you called it, it's probably a place with a large population of vampires. Someone there might have met them, might know where they went. My Uncle Glenn is dead. Uncle Terry will die any day now. When that happens, I'll be alone in the world, without a family. After the way I cut them off, that's what *I* deserve. But instead of torturing myself, I decided it was worth a shot to try and find them, to make things right. I at least want the chance to say I'm sorry for how I acted."

My heart ached for him. Studying his sorrowful face, I considered taking him with us to the Bastion. Someone there might actually know something about his parents.

But I dismissed the notion immediately. I couldn't take

Shane there. I was pretty sure even I wasn't welcome there, and humans certainly weren't.

"I wish I *could* bring you with us. But I can't."

He looked crestfallen. "Why not?"

"This place we're going is dangerous for you. I'm not sure I can adequately express *how* dangerous it is. There are thousands of vampires, and not a human for miles. You could be killed instantly upon arrival simply for being human."

"It's not like I have that much left to live for. As I said, I'm alone. I'm willing to take the chance."

"That's not all," I confessed. "I sort of... got thrown out."

"What, you? Miss Goody Goody? Don't tell me you broke the rules?"

"In a way. The ruler there ordered me to do something, and I refused. She banished me. The only reason we're going there now is we have no other place to turn. I need to get Kelly and Heather somewhere they'll be safe. And I need help to find out where my friend Larkin is. If she's been taken to a Safety Center, I have to get her out before something even worse happens to her. There are soldiers there who could help her."

Shane nodded gravely. "I understand. And I'll do whatever it takes to help you get home."

"Thank you," I whispered, feeling even more guilty now for saying no to his request. "Maybe I can still help you too. When I get there, I could ask around about your parents. If I find out anything, I could call you—that is, when you get a new phone."

His warm brown eyes filled with affection. "That'll be the very first thing I do when I get home. I would welcome a call from you—even if you don't have any information on them."

His voice softened. "Thank you for being willing to help me, Abigail."

"Thank you for being willing to help *us*."

He grinned. "Look at us... we're a mini Vampire-Human Coalition."

"I guess we are."

For a moment we sat smiling at each other.

Then there was a bang and a flash of light, and I screamed in pain.

24

A THING FOR VAMPIRE GIRLS

"Look out," Shane yelled.

Launching himself at me, he covered my body with his, blocking the sunlight that had hit me full blast and singed my skin and eyes. The plywood loft door creaked back and forth on its hinges in the wind.

A gust had blown it wide open, leaving a wide shaft of daylight stretching across the loft floor.

Shane's face above me contracted in concern. "Your forehead and nose are burned."

"All of me would have been burned if you hadn't moved so fast. Thank you."

He was still on top of me, breathing hard from adrenaline. Shane was a thin guy, but he was solidly built, and his body was heavier than I would have thought.

I let out a nervous giggle. "Vampires don't have to breathe much, but we do need *some* oxygen." At his quirked expression of confusion, I added, "You're crushing me."

"Oh. Right. Sorry about that." He lifted a little, propping his upper body on his elbows, which were planted on either side of my shoulders.

Not moving off me, he glanced back over his shoulder. "I'm not sure about what to do here. If I move to go shut the door, the sun will hit you."

"If it's just for a second, I'll be okay. My skin will heal. I can take the pain."

He shook off my assurance. "I never want anything to hurt you—even for a second."

In spite of my awkward discomfort, there was a strange sensation in my chest, a sort of thawing and softening that left it feeling tender.

At a loss for words, I simply said, "Thank you," again.

Shane lifted his head and scanned the loft area. "I was hoping there'd be an old blanket up here or something, but there's nothing. You think if we yell for Heather and Kelly one of them could help us?"

I crinkled my face in doubt. "Maybe. Once vampires fall asleep, we're pretty hard to wake. You remember that day in the truck on the way to San Francisco."

Making sure to stay in Shane's shadow, I twisted my neck to the side. "Heather. Kelly," I called out. "Wake up. I need help."

Nothing. My friends were not Bloodbound soldiers. They were just two regular girls who'd had a very long, stressful day and were exhausted.

When both mine and Shane's calls went unanswered, we looked at each other and laughed a little.

"I think we're on our own here," he said.

"Yep, and my legs are starting to fall asleep."

"Really?" He shifted his weight, taking more of it onto his knees, which bracketed mine.

"No, not really. But we can't stay like this all day long."

Shane gave me a rascally grin. "Oh, I don't know about

that. I'm pretty comfortable myself. I could at least stay here until the sun changes position."

"Or..." I said, "you could put your arm under me and drag me as you crawl forward until we're out of the light."

His delighted expression fell. "I'm more a fan of the stay-here-all-day plan, but you're right. That could work, too."

Bracing himself on one elbow and sliding the other arm beneath my waist, Shane began moving us both. We made progress by slow inches.

Each time he lifted me to pull me forward with him, the front of my body pressed against the front of his. One time, we knocked foreheads and both laughed.

But by the time we reached the safety of a shaded area, Shane was no longer laughing. His face appeared strained, and when he moved his arm from beneath me, he didn't roll off of me. Instead, he stared down into my eyes.

"I do want to find my parents," he whispered. "But even if I wasn't looking for them, I would still have wanted to help you."

I nodded. "I believe you. Can you... move?"

After another long look, he did, shifting his weight and rolling onto his back just next to me. For a moment, we lay side by side, breathing and recovering.

"I'm not sure where along the way this happened, but it's moved past guilt over my uncles' actions," Shane said. "Now it's much more than that. I care for you, Abigail. You know that by now, don't you?"

I sighed, looking up at the rafters instead of at his earnest face. "Why?"

My money was on the queen bee pheromones, but I couldn't tell him about that. Besides, I still didn't know if it even affected humans.

Shane pushed up on an elbow, rolling onto his side to

look down at my face. "What's that supposed to mean? There's all kinds of reasons why. You're smart, funny, sweet... and you're so beautiful you take my breath away."

The unexpected comment—and the absorbed expression he wore—stole *my* breath. "Do you... have a *thing* for vampire girls or something?"

His smile crashed. He looked hurt. "No. Well, maybe. But it's not just that. Is it so hard to believe I just like you? That I'm attracted to *you*?"

Yes. Because I let myself believe that about Reece, and it turned out I was laughably, tragically wrong.

"I don't know," I mumbled. "Shane... I don't know what to say."

For a long moment he just stared into my eyes. Then his gaze shifted to my lips. "You don't have to say anything," he whispered.

Before I knew what was happening, his mouth was on mine. At first, I was so shocked I didn't respond. And then I did.

The response probably wasn't the one Shane was looking for. My fangs emerged, and my stomach growled, my thirst roaring to life. He jerked back.

"Oh—I forgot about your blood addiction. Does kissing me bother you?"

Yes. But it wasn't for the reason he assumed. The second his lips touched mine, a vivid image of Reece had popped into my mind.

"Um... kind of. Listen, I have a confession to make. That story I told you about blood addiction? It *is* true... about some vampires, like Kelly. But not about me. There's another reason I wouldn't drink from you back at your uncle's house."

Shane's brows drew together. "What is it? Do I smell bad or something?"

A surprised laugh barked out of me. "What? No. Why would you ask that?"

"Well, Marjorie said some humans smell better than others. And some smell distinctly *un*appetizing."

I rocked my head back and forth. "No. You smell just fine. I didn't bite you—couldn't let myself bite you—because of what happened with Josiah."

"But I already told you I haven't been bitten that many times. I won't turn."

"I can't be sure of that. There's a chance that with me, it might take only one bite. I could never do that to another person—certainly not to you after all you've done for us. Believe me, you don't want this life. Especially now with the way things are going under President Parker. It's a really bad time to be a vampire."

He nodded in understanding and then he blushed deeply. "So then..." He stopped and swallowed. "If kissing me doesn't make you want to bite me... can I kiss you again?"

Sitting up, I scooted away from him. He sat up as well, and his mouth quirked with amusement. "I guess that's a 'no.'"

"Shane, I like you. Very much. You are truly a nice guy, and I can't thank you enough for helping us get this far, for keeping me from flame-broiling a few minutes ago. But I have a history that makes getting involved with anyone difficult."

"What happened with your friend Josiah doesn't bother me," he said. "You had just turned, you're remorseful about it, and I know you'd never hurt me."

"That's not the history I'm talking about. There's a guy. A vampire."

His hopeful expression changed into something resembling embarrassment. "Oh. I thought you said you didn't really date. Well actually you said there was a boyfriend once, but I thought it was in the past."

The word "boyfriend" seemed so trite, so inadequate to describe what Reece had been to me, but I didn't know what else to call him, so I didn't correct Shane.

"It is. It's over. He's... not available."

"I remember. You said he made an 'eternal commitment' to someone else."

"Yes. He did. But the fact he's not available doesn't change my feelings. I loved him. I still do."

Shane reached for my hand, taking it inside his own. "I get it. Just know that I'm here for you—as a friend. And if you ever feel ready for something more..."

I interrupted, fighting tears. "Thanks. We should both try to get some sleep. You've got to fly home tomorrow." *And I have to face Imogen.*

And Reece.

Giving me a tight smile, Shane said, "You're right. You three are making me nocturnal. I'm actually starting to get tired at dawn."

Turning away from the guy who wanted to be with me, I curled up on my side and thought of the one who didn't.

I wrapped my hand around the pendant that contained his blood, reliving some of the sweeter moments we'd shared, the way he'd looked at me, the times he'd held me... and kissed me.

What a mess I was. Reece probably never even thought of me anymore, and I was still so consumed with him I couldn't manage a simple kiss with another guy.

A familiar, deep ache echoed in my chest. How would I ever bring myself to move on with someone new?

No one was ever going to replace Reece in my heart.

Tomorrow I would see him again—if Imogen didn't kill me first for daring to return to the Bastion.

Either way, my homecoming was bound to be excruciating.

25

BEYOND MY EXPECTATIONS

At nightfall, we left the barn and the 18-wheeler behind.

Walking to my family's home, we passed scenery as familiar to me as the sight of my own hands. Rolling hills and pastures dotted with farmhouses and wooden farm buildings.

"It's really peaceful here," Kelly said, inhaling the scents around us—earth, evergreen boughs, chimney smoke. "It seems like such a nice place to grow up."

"It was, though I didn't appreciate it at the time," I confessed.

"I've gotta admit there's something to be said for being isolated from the rest of the world," Heather said. "This seems like just about the safest place on earth. Especially these days."

It had been—once. Not so much after I'd turned, and my father had told me to leave the community. How would he react to seeing me tonight? Would he reject me again and refuse to help us?

"Speaking of being isolated from the world, when we get

to the Bastion tonight, maybe I should go in alone first," I said. "If everything's okay, I'll come out and get you two."

Shane gave me an alert glance. "I thought you were going there to be *safe*. Is there some kind of danger to you at this place?"

"I'll be fine."

"As long as Imogen doesn't give the off-with-her-head order," Heather said.

Shane's expression changed from interest to anger. "Now hold on a minute. You told me you were thrown out. You didn't say anything about the death penalty for returning."

He shot a glance at Heather. "You *are* joking about that off-with-her-head thing, right?"

She scrunched up her face and shrugged her shoulders. "Not really."

Now Shane's gaze returned to me. "You can't go."

"I have to."

"Well then I'm going with you."

"No way. That would only make things worse," I said. "Plus, there's nothing you could do against a cavern full of vampires."

"I could try."

Once again, I got that soft, melty feeling in my chest. "Look, I appreciate the thought, but it's out of the question. It would be literal suicide for you. I'll be fine. In spite of her threats, I don't believe she'll actually do anything to me. Nothing permanent anyway. And we need a place to hide. It's not safe for us *outside* of the Bastion anymore."

Reaching the front door of my family's home, I hesitated before knocking, my heart doing a crazy dance in my chest.

It'll be okay. All they can say is no. You have to try. Your friends need help.

Still, if they treated me like a stranger, I didn't know how I was going to stand it.

Finally, I knocked. My youngest sister Rebecca opened the door. When she saw me, her eyes bulged then she smiled and threw her arms around me.

"Abigail! You're home. I missed you so much. We all have. Mamm has been so mad at Dad since you left. We all worried we'd never see you again."

Shocked by her exuberant welcome, it took me a minute to respond. "I missed you too. Is... is he here?"

I would not let myself get too excited about what Rebecca had said—that they'd missed me—until I saw my father's face. This happy reunion would come to an abrupt end if he wouldn't allow me in the house.

She pulled back and looked up at me. "He hasn't come in from the fields yet. I'll go and get Mamm. She's in the basement doing laundry."

She ran off, and a few moments later my mother appeared in the doorway at the top of the basement stairs. Her face reddened, and her eyes filled with tears when she saw me. Drawing me into her arms, she hugged me fiercely.

"My Abigail has returned. You are truly a sight for sore eyes. I haven't given your father a day's peace since he sent you away."

She released me and gave my outfit a quick once-over. Clearly, she disapproved, but she didn't say so. Instead, she smiled at my friends. "And who are these?"

"Mamm, I'd like you to meet Heather and Kelly and Shane."

She made a come-here gesture with both hands. "You're all welcome. Any friend of Abigail's is a friend of ours. Do come in out of the cold."

I hadn't noticed it being cold, but Shane stepped inside eagerly and headed for the fireplace.

"May I offer you all some water or tea? Or something to eat?" Mamm asked.

Kelly and Heather said, "No thank you." Shane took her up on the offer of both. I felt guilty, suddenly realizing how little he'd eaten during the past few days.

Mamm and I joined him at the table where he devoured a bowl of stew and then another. Heather and Kelly sat on the floor with Rebecca and my brother, Noah, and my youngest brother, Daniel, who had introduced my friends to his new kittens.

They all laughed together and chatted like old friends about the antics of the tiny creatures.

My mother took my hands inside hers. "How have you been, Abigail? I've worried for you, and I've prayed for you every morning and night."

My throat was instantly sore, and it was hard to speak around the lump lodged there. "I'm okay. It's been hard, but I have friends. We're there for each other."

Her face colored. "I feel sick that your family wasn't there for you. Your father did what he thought was best to protect us all at the time, but I know he regrets it. He prays for you too."

"He doesn't think I'm a demon?" I asked.

She shook her head. "None of us knew anything about vampires—not really. We were afraid because we were ignorant."

"Maybe you were right to be afraid. Look what happened with Josiah."

"No. We were ignorant. After that night when your father returned from the hospital without you, I insisted we read some library books on vampirism. We understand a lot more now. We're no longer afraid of you."

"Not even Dad?"

"Him least of all. One of the things he's prayed for is that you would return so he could apologize to you." She smiled. "I can't wait to see his face when he walks through that door."

I didn't want to get my hopes up, but I couldn't help it. I'd intended to ask them for the loan of a buggy to get us closer to the Bastion. A happy reunion with my family was so far above and beyond my expectations, I could hardly believe it was happening.

But when the door did open and my father came inside and saw me there, it was just as Mamm had said. His tired face crumpled, and he moved toward me, literally falling to his knees in front of the dining chair where I sat and reaching for my hands.

"Forgive me, daughter," he said in a choked voice. "I'm so sorry for what I did, and I'm happy to have the chance to tell you."

I shook my head, almost too choked up to speak. "Dad... it's okay. I understand. You were afraid."

"Have you come home to stay?" he asked, turning his head and apparently just now noticing the three strangers in his house.

"No. We're just passing through. I came to ask for help. We're in trouble. We're on our way to a safe place, but we need transportation."

"You must stay here," Mamm insisted. "This is a safe place. This is your home. And we want to hear about where you've been and what you've been doing all this time. We'll help you with whatever the trouble is."

"I'm afraid you can't."

Dad rose and pulled out the chair on the other side of me, joining us at the table. Shane stuck out his hand. "I'm Shane Eastwood. Nice to meet you, sir."

"It's nice to meet you, son." My father studied Shane's brown eyes then turned to me with a quizzical look. "Tell us what's happened."

I explained how Kelly and Heather and I had been falsely arrested and held at the Safety Center and how the circumstances of our escape had put us in grave danger.

"The Amish community can't help us now," I said. "And I wouldn't want to bring suspicion on you and Mamm and get you in trouble with the law for harboring fugitives."

"Are you a foo-ji-tive too, Shane?" five-year-old Daniel asked, clearly enthralled by the exotic sound of the word.

Shane shook his head. "No. I'm just trying to help Abigail and her friends."

"She's a vampire now," Daniel announced. "But that doesn't mean she's bad."

Shane grinned and riffled the much younger boy's hair. "I know that. I'm glad you do too."

"Thank you for helping my daughter. You're a good man," Dad said.

Shane ducked his head, looking embarrassed by the praise. "Just trying to do what's right, sir. Also, I'm looking for my parents who are vampires, so Abigail is helping me as much as I'm helping her. Hopefully we'll be able to heal our relationship too."

My father nodded gravely. "There's nothing more important than family. I hope you find them."

We spent the next hour catching up before I had to regretfully announce it was time to go.

"Can't you stay just one more day?" Mamm pleaded.

"Each day that passes increases the chances we're caught

here," I said. "I can't have that happen. And Shane has to get back home to California. We need to get to the vampire stronghold before daybreak."

Dad pushed back from the table. "Noah and I will hitch up the horses to the old buggy. I was about to pass it down to him since we recently got a new one. You may take it and return it when you can."

"I have a friend where I'm going who can arrange to return it to you," I said, thinking of Kannon. He was familiar with the area and the location of my village. I could give him directions to my family farm when we reached the Bastion.

"No need," Dad assured me. "I have a friend who owns a farm very near to the highway just over the state line. If you leave the buggy and horses with him, he'll see to it they get home again."

"Thank you. And thank you for the clothes, Mamm— and your hospitality."

She had asked my sister Rachel to find some plain clothes for each of us to wear as we traveled the rest of the way. They would complete the illusion that would hopefully keep us from being recognized during the rest of our journey.

"I only wish I was able to feed you and the other girls," Mamm said. "But I understand why I can't. At least I was able to meet your young man and fatten him up."

She patted Shane's shoulder and cleared his empty plate and bowl.

"Oh—no—we uh... we're just friends," I told her, but he winked at me.

"You can fatten me up anytime, Mrs. Byler."

"Come back anytime," she said. "All of you."

Thirty minutes later we were hugging goodbye at the door, and I was promising my siblings to return soon or at least to write. Daniel wrapped his arms around the long skirt that covered my legs to the ankles.

"I wish I could come with you to the vampire house," he said with a pout.

I knelt so we were face to face. "I wish you could come too. But it's very far, and Dad needs your help here on the farm. I'll try to come back soon, okay? You be good until then."

He nodded and hugged my neck, sniffling a little, which brought tears to my eyes. I hoped what I'd said to my family was true, that I'd be *able* to return.

I really didn't know *what* would happen when we reached the Bastion or if I'd ever see them again.

Pulling the buggy away from the house, I at least felt reasonably sure we'd make it there safely without any further interruption.

26

SISTERS

"You know, this getup is surprisingly comfortable," Heather said from the back seat of the buggy. "I might start wearing Amish clothes all the time. I'd never have to worry about shaving my legs again. Or holding in my stomach."

Kelly laughed. "Or doing your hair. Just throw on a bonnet and go."

I twisted back so I could see them past my own traveling bonnet, which blocked my side view. It was strange to be in plain clothes again, driving a horse-drawn buggy. Dad said the team of horses could easily take us to the state line. From there we would go on foot.

"Well, I don't think I could ever get used to pants with no zipper," Shane quipped. "And I'm not sure I'm a hat guy."

"It looks good on you," I assured him. "You look very Amish. It's a good thing we *didn't* stay another day. One of my sisters might have snapped you up if you walked around dressed like that."

He beamed, a wicked gleam in his eye. "Would that bother you?"

His flirty question caught me off guard. "Of course not. I would be glad for you to find someone to make you happy."

"*You* make me happy," he insisted.

I turned away and focused on the reins, willing my hands not to shake as I held them. As the miles passed, my heart grew heavier and heavier. It seemed impossible that after all we'd been through, we'd be going our separate ways in just a few hours.

At least I knew he'd be okay. If the authorities discovered he'd been with us, he could simply tell them we'd kidnapped him and forced him to travel with us.

No doubt they'd find it an easy story to believe. It was what they *wanted* to believe.

When we spotted the Virginia state line checkpoint in the distance, Shane and I switched places, though I still kept control of the reins.

If we were a real Amish family, he'd be doing the driving as the male. I didn't want to raise any suspicions with the border agents.

I turned to my friends in the back seat. "Pretend to be asleep. Close your eyes and turn your heads to the sides so the bonnets will shield your faces."

"Most of these guys are half-asleep anyway," Shane said. "Or deeply involved in playing war games on their phones. They'll probably just wave us through. An Amish buggy is the last place they'll be looking for vampires."

"I hope you're right. I lost one of my contact lenses. I'll just keep my head down. You'll have to do the talking anyway, as the *man*—otherwise it would look suspicious," I said.

Apparently, my worry was for nothing. When we reached the agent's hut, the guy on duty looked drowsy and bored. He rose from his stool and stretched before lumbering to the curb.

He pressed the button to raise the bar before even speaking to us. Obviously knowing Amish people didn't have driver's licenses, he didn't ask for one.

"Good evening folks. You're out awfully late," he said in a friendly tone.

I focused on my hands folded in my lap as Shane answered and gave him the story we'd agreed upon.

"Yes, sir. My sisters and I were visiting our cousins in Elkins, and we let the time get away from us. Chores to do in the morning though."

The guy chuckled. "Those chickens and cows don't like waiting for their breakfast, do they? Grew up on a farm myself in Hickory."

Shane nodded. "Nice place."

The guard's expression quirked. "You've been to North Carolina? You folks don't usually roam that far."

"Oh, I thought you meant the Hickory in Virginia." Shane pivoted, sounding nervous now. Having grown up in California, he wasn't familiar with the town names in this area.

The agent must have noticed the quiver in his voice because his expression grew more alert. Taking the flashlight from his belt, he shone it into the buggy's back seat.

The beam passed over the dark clothes and black bonnets Kelly and Heather wore. They remained motionless with their faces hidden, feigning sleep.

"Three sisters, huh?" The agent's tone was less friendly now and more wary.

The fingers in my lap twisted together, and I did a little mental self-talk to keep my fangs from emerging.

It's okay, He doesn't know anything. He's just making conversation. Don't panic.

"Lucky me," Shane said. "The twins finally conked out and stopped chattering. This one's the quiet one." He hooked his thumb toward me.

"And how are you tonight, ma'am?" the guard asked.

Wonderful. Why had Shane referred to me? Now I would be obligated to speak to him.

Keeping my head bowed, I said, "Very well, sir. Thank you."

"I told you. She's shy," Shane said.

For a moment, the agent was silent. Then he stepped back onto the curb and twisted his head to the side, speaking into a radio attached to his collar. "This is Agent Eggleston at checkpoint forty-eight. I've got a possible 9-8-6."

Uh oh. I had no idea what a 9-8-6 was, but it couldn't be good.

Speaking to Shane again, the man asked, "You kids seen anything suspicious on the road? Groups of people out walking in the dark or anything like that?"

Shane's voice was even shakier now. "No, sir. Nothing out of the ordinary."

"Well, you should keep an eye out and be careful. There's a large vampire population in Virginia, and one of our agents at a checkpoint in Pennsylvania reported a female vamp traveling with a young human male in a trailer truck. They were headed this direction."

"Is that unusual?"

The guard rested his hand on his gun holster. "There was a breakout at a Safety Center in California a few days ago. Hundreds of vampires escaped. Some guards were killed. One was kidnapped and murdered by three females.

That Pennsylvania agent said the little blonde vamp in the truck was a pretty good match for one of the killers. He suspected she might have been manipulating the human guy she was with. They do that sort of thing, you know."

"Well, thank you for the warning," Shane said. "I wish you a good night. Stay safe."

He lifted the reins in preparation to depart, but the agent held up a hand. "Just a minute. Would you mind removing your bonnet, ma'am?"

27

CALLING IN THE CAVALRY

orry bored through my midsection like the auger my father used to dig post holes on our farm.

"That is against our religion," I said to Agent Eggleston, leaning heavily into the Pennsylvania Dutch accent of my childhood. "You must know that."

"I'm sorry, but it's regulations ma'am." His tone was respectful but firm. He wasn't going to back down on this.

Without a word, I nodded and untied the strings beneath my chin, pulling the traveling bonnet from my head. Dark hair spilled down my back.

Though it had been cut since I'd left my Amish community, it was still quite long, adhering to the style of Amish women.

The agent's sigh of relief was audible. I wasn't blonde. The problem was, Kelly was feet away from him, and I suspected she was a *perfect* match to the description he and all the state border agents had been given.

"Thank you, ma'am. You can put that back on," Agent Eggleston said. "I just need to do a temp check on all of you, and then you can be on your way. It'll just take a sec."

"Must you wake my sisters?" Shane asked. He was beginning to panic. I could hear his heart pounding.

"It'll just take a sec," the agent repeated.

I had to do something. If he wanded all of us and discovered three out of the four "Amish siblings" in the buggy were vampires, the ruse would be up. He'd detain us for sure, and it would take only a quick internet search to match Kelly, Heather, and me to our mug shots.

We'd be sent back to prison—or more likely executed—for "murdering" a guard.

Not for the first time, I wished I really did have the power to mesmerize a human. It would have come in very handy.

As it was, I'd have to rely on my wits.

"That is not our way, sir." I kept my eyes down but spoke loudly and clearly. "Your modern technology is against our beliefs."

"I'm afraid it is *our* way ma'am. And if you want to enjoy our 'modern' highways, you have to abide by the law of the land," he said.

I nodded. "I understand."

We were going to have to take him out, overpower him and lock him up without his radio so he couldn't call for backup—unless he'd done that already with that 9-8-6 code.

The other option was to abandon the buggy—and Shane—and make a run for it. We were *so close* to the Bastion now. We simply couldn't allow ourselves to be captured after making it this far.

But how could I leave Shane? I'd promised to help him find his parents. Worse, he might be in legal trouble for traveling with us. He'd have a hard time claiming he'd been kidnapped and forced now that he'd lied to the agent.

The man held his electronic thermometer to Shane's

forehead, and it beeped. I could tell from the agent's low grunt he was satisfied with the readout. It was my turn.

Slowly I turned toward him. My eyes were shaded by the bonnet, but it didn't matter now if he saw their color. The second he read my temperature he'd know I wasn't human.

When he extended the wand toward me, I grabbed his wrist and sprang from the buggy, pulling his arm around behind his back.

"Hey," he yelled. "You can't do that. I'm an officer of the law."

"I'm sorry. We're not going to hurt you," I said as I reached for his other wrist. But it was too late. He'd already gotten a hand on his gun.

Drawing it, he raised the weapon over his head, angling it down behind his back toward me and pulling the trigger. Red-hot pain sliced through my left thigh. A couple feet higher and the platinum bullet would have pierced my heart, ending my life.

The heat at the entry wound morphed to aching cold, which was spreading rapidly down toward my knee and up toward my hip. I couldn't let the agent get off another round, but it was impossible to stay on my feet.

As I fell, I grabbed for his gun hand, but he spun away, turning to face me with his weapon aimed at my chest.

He spoke into the radio clipped to his collar, calling for backup and describing us and our vehicle.

I lifted a hand toward him. "Please. We're not dangerous. Just let my friends go."

"Shut up," he ordered. "Don't move an inch. I *will* shoot you through the heart."

"Abigail!" Shane yelled.

I darted at glance at him standing horror-struck in the buggy's open front. "No! Stay back. You'll get hurt."

He didn't listen to me. Leaping from the buggy, Shane landed on the agent's back, knocking him to the ground where the two of them rolled and grappled for control of the agent's weapon.

It fired again, a loud crack that echoed for several seconds.

Shane collapsed.

"No. Oh no."

I crawled toward him while Kelly and Heather leapt from the buggy to subdue the agent. Each gripped one of his arms.

Shane writhed on the asphalt, which was becoming soaked with his blood. I had to hold my breath to suppress a surge of thirst.

"Where were you hit? Can you tell me? Can you speak?"

Moaning and gasping for breath, he didn't answer, just shook his head, squinting in pain and clutching his mid-section.

"Abbi—we need to get out of here," Heather said. "I hear sirens."

"I hear them, too," Kelly said. They both sounded terrified.

Sure enough, the wail of sirens filled the air. Lifting my head, I saw a police car speeding our way, lights flashing.

The agent barked a harsh laugh. "You're screwed now. I called it in before you jumped me. You're the escapees, aren't you? Don't matter if you run now—we're going to get you sooner or later. And that bullet you took contains liquid platinum. It's working its way through your veins toward your heart right now. You've got about five minutes left to live, little vamp—less if you run and speed up your heart rate."

I looked over at Shane again, who was insensible with pain at this point, then back up at my friends.

"You two go. Run home. I can't leave him to die here alone."

"We can't leave *you*," Kelly said.

"Yes—you can. You have to. Go. Get to safety. You can't help me. Tell Kannon what happened. Tell..." *Reece* "...them... I didn't make it."

"Abbi..." Heather whined. She and Kelly stood looking at me with anguished faces.

The car was nearly upon us. Any second now the officers would jump out, guns drawn, and my friends would be arrested.

"Go," I repeated in a louder voice. "Go. Please. I love you."

They disappeared into the darkness outside the checkpoint's lights just before the squad car braked in front of me and Shane.

Two police officers got out of the car. They did indeed have their guns drawn, and both were shouting for me to lie down on my belly.

My leg was aching and ice cold now. Moving it was agony, but I complied. The instant I was down, one of them jerked my arms behind me and locked a pair of platinum handcuffs around my wrists.

"The other two ran off. Headed east." The border agent sounded out of breath. "You might be able to catch them."

One of the officers, who looked about fifty years old and about fifty pounds over his ideal weight, said, "They're vampires. We can't catch them. But we've got *her*, and she's going to tell us where they went—and anything else we want to know, aren't you sweetheart?"

He gave my injured thigh a little kick, causing me to cry out in pain.

"You might want to get her to a hospital if you want to question her," the agent said. "I shot her with one of those new exploding rounds. She's full of platinum, probably won't last too much longer."

"Dammit. All right. We'll have to radio the trauma center, but it's ninety miles away. Hopefully she won't croak in the car."

"Please help him," I begged. Shane was unconscious now, and by the look and smell of things was losing blood at an alarming rate.

"We'll consider it... as long as you're cooperative," the other, much younger, officer said. "What is he, your own personal blood donor?"

The two officers and the border agent all chuckled, which infuriated me.

"He's my friend. I don't drink from humans."

"Sure you don't," the older officer said.

"That's what they all say when they're arrested," his partner said. "Their victims tell another story. Okay, let's get a move on. Put her in the back."

"What about him?" I asked, nearly in a panic now over Shane's condition—which no one but me seemed to really care about.

The younger officer sneered. "Don't worry. I'll call an ambulance from the car. They'll come scoop up your little vamp-loving 'friend' and take him to the hospital. Say your goodbyes now. Where you're going, you won't be seeing him for a *long* time."

He yanked me up and started dragging me toward the police cruiser but paused as a large, black tactical unit van pulled up.

"You gotta be kidding me." The older officer shot a look of disbelief at the border agent. "You called for a SWAT unit? Little bit of overkill calling in the cavalry, don't you think?"

The agent shook his head in obvious confusion. "I told dispatch there were three of them. I don't know why they sent SWAT."

The doors on both sides of the armored vehicle opened, and a swarm of uniformed men poured out.

They were not wearing SWAT uniforms.

Not police or military uniforms either.

They wore the distinctive black leather of the Bloodbound.

28

———

SOUP'S ON

The police officers stared at them in bafflement.

"Who are you guys?" the young officer asked. "VSU?"

I'd heard of Vampire Suppression Units being formed in some of the larger cities. They were like SWAT teams for dealing with vampire threats.

Unfortunately for the officers, this particular unit was the exact opposite—and the humans were severely outnumbered.

Before they had a chance to figure that out and even raise a weapon, they were all dead, either beheaded or run through with a wicked Bloodbound sword.

Blood was everywhere now, and the vampire warriors weren't going to let it go to waste.

"Soup's on, boys," one of them called out in a jovial tone.

"Make sure you drain them completely," another cautioned. "These guys would make crappy vampires."

I sat and watched the scene in a state of semi-shock, not sure if I should thank them or scream. It had been a while since I'd been around Bloodbound warriors. I'd forgotten how big and intimidating they were.

When a couple of the men moved toward Shane's helpless, still form, I snapped out of my fugue.

"Stop," I yelled. "Not him."

Halting their progress, they looked back at me. "Why not? It's a waste of good blood to just let it all spill out on the cement."

"He's with me. I'm taking him to the Bastion."

They exchanged amused glances. One of them laughed out loud. "You mean as a snack, right? There's no Inception Ceremony coming up."

None of them looked familiar. They must have been new recruits to the Bloodbound ranks. Who knew how many the brotherhood numbered by now?

Was Reece among them? I didn't see him. Perhaps he ranked too highly at this point to be sent out on routine patrols.

That had to be what this was—there was no way Kelly and Heather had made it to the Bastion quickly enough to send help.

"I'm Abigail Byler," I said to the guys who were once again moving toward Shane.

Desperate to convince them to spare his life, I mustered as much dignity as I could from my position bleeding on the ground. "Imogen's daughter."

"They know who you are," someone said from behind me. "Why do you think we're here?"

My head jerked around at the familiar voice. "Kannon!"

If I hadn't been crippled and in excruciating pain, I'd have flung myself at my old friend and hugged him. It was incredibly good to see his handsome Viking face. Spotting my injury, he hurried toward me, wrapping an arm around my back to pull me up to my good leg.

"What the *hell* are you doing here, squirt? I thought you were out in California with all the peace-loving hippies now."

I sagged against him, grateful for the support. "I was. But then... well, it's a long story, which I'll be happy to tell you later. Right now I need to get some help for my friend."

"Looks like you need help yourself. You've been shot. What kind of round was it?"

"Don't worry about me. You don't happen to have any O-negative in that truck, do you?"

"Thirsty?"

"No—not for me. For him. He's lost a lot of blood. It's the universal donor type."

"No, but we've got some back at the Bastion, of course. You can't really mean to take a human there, though."

"Yes. I do. He helped me and Kelly and Heather escape from a bad situation. He got us here. I can't just leave him here to die. He needs help, Kannon. The hospital's too far away—he won't make it. I have to get him to Dr. Coppa."

He peered around me to check out Shane's body lying in a pool of blood. "I'm not sure he'll make it to the Bastion either. He looks pretty far gone. Sure you don't want to just turn him?"

I fought off another flare of thirst. "Absolutely sure. Can you help me get him into the truck?"

Kannon's face creased in consternation as he glanced around at the brightly lit border station. At the moment, it looked like a massacre scene.

"Yeah, okay, but she's not going to be happy about this."

She. Imogen. Chill bumps rose on my skin and lifted the fine hairs on my arms.

"I know. Thank you for doing it anyway."

After another reluctant glance down at me, Kannon helped me to the van then went back to scoop my human friend off the pavement.

Shane woke. "Ow. Shit that hurts. Abigail?" He twisted his head, searching for me.

I called out to him from the van's open rear door. "Right here. We're taking you somewhere to get you some help."

"Or to get him eaten," Kannon muttered.

"What?" Shane whipped his head back and forth as he surveyed the bloody aftermath. "What's happening?"

Kannon didn't bother to answer but placed Shane on the floor of the van next to me. "Just be still, kid. You're getting blood on the carpet, and you don't have that much left to spare."

To the other Bloodbound, Kannon barked out orders. "Clean this place up. Dispose of the bodies. Destroy the cameras and recordings. Remove any trace of yourselves or of Abigail and her friends. Meet back at the Bastion—and one of you bring along the buggy and horses. I'm going on ahead."

He slid the back door closed then got behind the wheel of the enormous vehicle, starting it and putting it into gear. I looked around the rear section and found a leather jacket someone had left behind on the floor. Balling it up, I pressed it against Shane's wound to stem the flow of fragrant fresh blood.

"Owwww," he groaned.

"Sorry. I can't have you bleeding out before we even get there."

"Where are we going?" he mumbled, nearly incoherent.

"Never mind. Just lie still and be quiet. You're going to be okay."

Kannon turned his head to the side for a second, taking his eyes off the road, though he was driving at blistering speed.

"How are *you* doing? You didn't say what kind of round you got hit with."

I grimaced. The icy pain had crept up over my hip and was now engulfing my stomach. I hadn't wanted to mention it, needing to get some help for Shane before I lost consciousness. I feared for his fate if I died before we got him to Dr. Coppa.

"The agent who shot me said it was platinum, some new exploding kind."

"What?" Kannon roared.

He jerked the wheel and caused the van to veer across the road before correcting it. "You should have told me right away. You need some vampire blood—now."

Would that heal me? Dr. Coppa had given Reece injections of small amounts of vampire blood when he was recovering from animal blood poisoning, but it hadn't occurred to me that vampire blood could save me from the liquid platinum infecting my bloodstream now.

Hope lifted my heart. Maybe I *hadn't* seen my friends for the last time. I could still help Shane.

And I would see Reece again.

It was stupid, but the thought was there anyway, undeniable and invigorating.

"Dammit. We're still thirty miles from the Bastion." Kannon added another, more colorful, swear, slamming a large hand against the steering wheel.

"Does it have to be injected?" I asked, confused. "Or are you worried you won't be able to drive while I drink from your arm?"

I'd never bitten anyone but Josiah and had sworn never

to bite a human again, but drinking from a vampire seemed tolerable. After all, I couldn't ruin a vampire's life with a single bite.

And I had no doubt Kannon would be willing to give me his blood if it would save my life. He'd been a good friend to me since the day we'd met.

"It's not that." His face in the rearview mirror twisted with dismay. "Our vows state that we'll never share our blood with anyone but Imogen."

"Really?"

The sacred Bloodbound vows weren't public knowledge, so it shouldn't have come as a surprise that I hadn't been aware of this one. It was just that... Reece had given me *his* blood on the day I'd left the Bastion.

Why?

29

ONE MORE LOOK

My hand went to the pendant on my chest, wrapping around it as it had so many times during the past year. I'd never been able to figure out why Reece had given the token to me. And now... knowing that he'd broken his vows to do so...

That's when it hit me. *Reece's blood.*

Drawing the chain over my head, I studied the miniature dagger and the orb at its hilt, which contained the swirling red essence of the love of my life.

Then I looked at Shane lying beside me. He groaned in pain. In spite of the piteous sight, hope danced in my chest.

"Kannon... would drinking vampire blood heal a human?"

"Don't even think about it," he said. "It doesn't work for them. Even if it did, you're too sick to give anyone your blood, much less a human. You should be drinking *his* to strengthen yourself."

"You know I can't do that."

"Yeah, because Sadie Aldritch has your thinking all twisted around backward. Just rest and hang on. We're only fifteen miles away now. Be as still as possible. The more you move, the faster that platinum will reach your heart."

I stopped talking and did as he said, but I could literally feel the poison creeping toward my chest like a killing frost. I wasn't going to make it to the Bastion.

Gripping the pendant, I considered my options. The blood inside the orb might be enough to save my life. But it was Reece's blood. If I drank it, *his* life would be in danger. He'd broken the Bloodbound vows by giving it to me.

But no one knows that. No one but me and him.

One problem... Kannon knew how grave my wound was. If I miraculously healed, he'd be suspicious.

I hesitated another few moments until the sensation of paralyzing cold reached my lungs and stole my breath.

Hearing my gasp, Kannon cast another worried glance in my direction. "Hang on. Just ten more miles."

I nodded in return, unable to answer.

It was now or never. I could let it all end here. I could close my eyes and let go of life, hoping the next, far better one my lifelong Amish beliefs had promised me would be waiting.

My gaze fell to Shane's face and the still-spreading red stain on his torso. If I died, there would be no reason for anyone at the Bastion to help him.

As nice as he was to me, Kannon wasn't a human-lover. He'd either leave Shane outside or let his Bloodbound brothers finish the human guy off.

And then I saw another face—this one perfectly preserved in my mind's eye. The strong brow bone, the intense lilac eyes shaded by thick, black hair.

It was pointless except for as an exercise in self torture, but God help me, I *wanted* one more look at him.

Raising the pendant's glass orb to my lips, I bit down on

it and cracked the surface, sucking the fluid from inside it into my mouth.

The last time I'd tasted blood, it had been human—Josiah's. Reece's blood was different—and infinitely better. The moment I tasted it, the pain around my heart ceased. The cold in my lungs began to recede like a wave drawing back from the shore, leaving warmth and comfort in its wake.

The weakness that had overcome my body began to ebb as well, and a new strength and energy filled me.

It had worked. Steadily the eerie cold sensation drained from my torso, retreating down my hip and leg to the point of the injury and then disappearing altogether.

Almost in disbelief, I shook my leg, flexed the thigh muscle then released it. It didn't feel as good as new. It felt better.

Kannon parked in the paved lot near the cavern's entrance then bounded out of the driver's seat and slid open the rear compartment's door. He reached for me as if to lift me, but I protested.

"Take him. I'm fine."

"You're not fine. You were shot with an exploding round. You're likely half-dead by now if not more, so don't try to be a hero. I'll help your human—*after* I help you."

"Kannon. I'm fine. I promise."

I rose to my feet, lifting each leg and moving it around to show him I was telling the truth. Then I jumped from the van to the ground, landing lightly without any sign of pain.

"See? I'm good."

"How is that possible?" Kannon demanded. "You couldn't even stand back at the checkpoint."

I shrugged. "I guess it was only a flesh wound. The bullet must have just grazed me instead of exploding inside me."

It was a lie, but a necessary one. The truth would get Reece punished if not killed. Knowing it would only put Kannon in a tough spot. To erase any doubt, I lifted the long skirt I wore and showed him the nearly healed wound on my lower thigh.

He stared at it for a second then, apparently satisfied, moved to lift Shane. "Okay, I guess you're right. All I can say is thank God because I've never seen anyone survive one of those rounds. I was really afraid you weren't going to get the chance to 'meet your maker' again. And she is *definitely* going to want to see you."

He looked down at Shane, whom he carried unconscious in his arms like a sleeping baby as we walked toward the entrance to the Bastion.

"As for you, my little human friend... you might end up wishing you'd never met her. I still don't know about this, Abbi..."

"You let me worry about her. Just get Shane to the medical clinic." Remembering something Kannon had said earlier, I asked, "How did you know where we were? You said you went there to get me?"

He nodded. "We monitor police radio. I overheard the border agent's call about three fugitive vampires at the checkpoint. When he said they were dressed as Amish and driving a buggy, I knew something was up. Besides... your mother has a sense about these things. She's the one who ordered us there in force."

"Your mother?" Shane said in a groggy voice. I'd thought he was completely out. Either he'd just come to or he'd been listening all along. "I thought your mom was Amish."

"Um... yeah. She is. I also have a vampire mother, the woman who turned me. She's the one who banished me."

30

MISTAKEN ASSUMPTION

It was hard to say which made me more nervous, the prospect of seeing Imogen again—or seeing Reece.

"How is he?" I asked Kannon as we descended the multi-level staircase leading to the series of connecting caverns that made up the Bastion.

Taking a moment to observe the injured human in his arms, he responded, "He's still breathing."

"No—not him," I said. "Though, yes, that's good."

I *should* have been asking about Shane. Instead my mind had been full of Reece.

While I'd been away, I'd missed many of the people who lived here, but Reece was the only one I'd thought of daily—hourly if I was being completely honest.

Though we hadn't seen each other or spoken at all since I left, he'd been with me every single day, no matter where I was. I wasn't sure if it was a vampire thing or something else, but he was always at the top of my mind.

That was why I'd never managed to move on, to develop any interest in any other guy—except for perhaps my budding friendship with Shane.

"Oh, you mean *him* him," Kannon said. "Reece is Reece. As stubborn and surly as ever. He's done well with the Bloodbound. Imogen's very pleased with him."

I'll bet she is.

Acid curdled in my belly as unpleasant memories from my last day at the Bastion flooded my mind. Reece kneeling at Imogen's side as she fondled his neck and shoulders and ran her fingers through his hair. The possessiveness in her touch. The subservient, defeated way *he* acted.

I didn't think I could stand to see a repeat performance. I'd have to see *her*, of course, but maybe it would be better to steer clear of Reece altogether during my time here, however long that might be.

We entered the first cavern, and all heads turned in our direction. No doubt the smell of Shane's flowing blood had gotten their attention. Several pairs of fangs emerged on the vampires closest to us. I was surprised no one licked their lips.

Kannon shot them intimidating glares, and they turned away. The crowd divided, stepping out of his path. I followed close behind as he led the way toward the medical clinic, holding Shane like a father protecting his toddler from vicious dogs.

This had been a mistake. Even if Dr. Coppa managed to heal Shane's wounds, I wasn't sure how I'd ever get him out of this place alive. We should have dropped him off at an airport earlier in our trip instead of keeping him with us this long.

It was my fault. I'd let myself get attached and make promises I wouldn't be able to keep. First Josiah, then Reece, and now Shane.

Every guy who'd gotten involved with me had ended up hurt—or worse.

I really *was* like my killer bee ancestors, like the queens who'd come before me.

Like Imogen.

We were in the tunnel leading to the medical clinic, nearly at its door, when the silhouette of an exceptionally tall man detached itself from the other shadows and blocked the corridor. I would have known him anywhere, even from his shape alone.

Reece.

My heart went into an instant frenzy, pumping my body full of adrenaline and sweltering heat.

Rather than providing fight-or-flight energy, it was paralyzing. I stopped in place, even as Kannon continued on toward him.

It was hard to look at Reece directly. Not only was I overcome with emotion, but his handsomeness was almost disorienting—like looking into an overly bright light that blinds you and leaves you seeing stars. It took everything I had just to keep breathing.

Had he actually gotten *better* looking or had I just forgotten how beautiful he was? Impossibly he seemed to have grown even larger, towering over me, his shoulders nearly spanning the corridor.

With his black hair, black Bloodbound uniform, and dark, brooding expression, he looked like every human's nightmare of a dangerous vampire male. But the sinful, full lips and turbulent violet eyes made him the stuff of another kind of dream—the kind *I* had about him almost nightly.

Those eyes roamed over me, cataloguing my traditional Amish clothing, my hair, checking every limb as if searching for damage. They stopped and lingered on the blood staining my skirt.

"Hello Reece," I managed to wheeze.

He didn't return my greeting. Instead, he smirked. "I see reports of your demise were somewhat premature. Heather and Kelly said you'd been shot. They said it was an exploding round."

"Yes. I... I guess it was only a flesh wound. A close call." Aware of Kannon's listening ears nearby, I didn't tell Reece his blood gift had saved my life.

He nodded in apparent acceptance, but his attention dropped to my pendant, to its cracked and empty glass orb. Then his intense gaze lifted to bore into mine.

He said nothing about the broken necklace. And he didn't say he was glad I was alive. In fact, he looked—and sounded—furious.

"What *can* you be thinking coming back here?"

The snark in his tone stung, but it did wonders for my shattered nerves, sparking a defiant anger that settled them instantly.

"Well it's *nice* to see you, too. The Bastion is a refuge for vampires in trouble, is it not? I'm in trouble. I didn't know where else to go."

His expression softened into something resembling reluctant concern. "What kind of trouble?"

"My friends and I are wanted by the authorities."

Reece shot a disdainful glance at Shane passed out in Kannon's arms. "Friends? All I see is a half-dead human."

"I meant Kelly and Heather. And yes, Shane *is* my friend—and yes, he's a human—who's hurt as you can see. He needs immediate medical attention, so if you'll please let us pass..."

Reece didn't move, just stood staring down at me. "Still a human-loving do-gooder, I see. That doesn't explain why you brought him *here*. If his injuries don't kill him, which based on the smell of things they will, then some thirsty

Bastion citizen will do the job. Probably the good doctor himself. Either way, I seriously doubt Shawn will make it through the night."

"His name is *Shane*—and I'm going to at least *try* to save him. Unlike you, I don't give up on the people I care about."

Fire flashed in Reece's eyes, and he stepped forward, gripping my shoulder and dragging me closer to him. Our eyes held intense contact as he spoke, his lips barely inches from mine.

"If you've fallen in love with this weak human, you're even more foolish than I thought you were. Whether he lives or dies, it won't last, you know."

I was too angry to contradict his mistaken assumption. "My feelings for him are none of your business. You made sure of that when you took the Bloodbound vows. Now please let us by."

"Yeah dude—this kid's skinny, but he's got heavy bones or something," Kannon added.

Reece stared down at me a moment longer then exhaled harshly and stepped aside.

"Get him settled and come right back out," he ordered. "I'm supposed to take you to Imogen."

31

WHAT OTHER REASON

Inside the clinic, some of the staffers said hello and expressed surprise at seeing me again.

They were even more surprised when they got a look at whom I'd brought with me. A tech left the room and returned quickly with Dr. Coppa.

"Abigail," he exclaimed. "I'm delighted to see you."

Then he picked up the scent of human blood. His fangs emerged.

Laughing in an embarrassed way, he covered his mouth with one hand. "Sorry. It's been a while since I was exposed to blood fresh from the vein. What's going on Abigail? Why have you brought him here?"

"He was shot while helping me and my friends get here. He's lost a lot of blood. I was hoping you could help him."

The doctor nodded. "Well, we have a large supply of blood bags on hand as well as the equipment to give him the infusions. But the bullet will need to be removed. It's been a long time since I worked in a human operating room. His... blood... may be an issue for me and my assistants. *If* he makes it through surgery, I'll have to isolate him here away from the general population while he recovers—for his own safety."

"I understand. And I know you can do it. I trust you."

"Who is he?"

"My friend, Shane Eastwood. He saved my life and Kelly's and Heather's lives too. I owe him. Please try. And don't let anything happen to him. He's important to me."

"Very well. Kannon, follow me. We'll put him in this first room on the right."

The doctor started calling out orders to the clinic staff. Once I saw Shane settled into a bed and hooked up to an IV, I headed for the clinic exit.

"Where are you going?" Dr. Coppa asked.

"To face the music. Imogen wants to see me."

THE SILENCE between us was deafening as Reece and I walked through the Bastion's connected caverns toward the throne room.

Though I hadn't expected a parade upon my return, it hurt that he would treat me so coldly, acting like I was a stranger instead of someone he'd once cared about.

Clearly he hadn't missed me the way I'd missed him. What a fool I'd been to keep pining away for him when he'd so obviously moved on.

"You haven't said anything about the fact I broke the pendant and drank your blood."

There was a beat before he answered.

"Your leg is covered in blood. Your blood. So I'm assuming the gunshot *didn't* graze you but penetrated your leg. Which means you did what you had to do."

He went on in a nonchalant tone. "It was an emergency. That's why I gave it to you—in case of emergency."

"Is that the only reason?"

He darted a side glance at me. "What other reason would there be?"

Because you cared. Because you missed me. Because you wanted a part of you to go with me, just as a part of me was left here with you.

Those were the reasons I'd been hoping to hear, but clearly I'd been way off in my wild imaginings about what the gift could have meant.

I didn't answer his question. Instead I asked him another one.

"Why are you angry that I've come back?"

His jaw worked side to side, and his lips twisted. Finally, he spoke. "I'm not angry. I have no particular feelings about it whatsoever. I'm merely curious... as to what could have made you think this place is safer for you than the outside world. Than *anywhere* else in the world."

Oof. It was like a punch in the gut that knocked all the air from my lungs. No feelings whatsoever?

"Believe me, I never intended to come back," I snapped. "I'm well aware *no one* wants me here. What can I say? I was desperate."

He didn't slow his pace. "You should know, things have changed since you left."

"Oh really? So you're *not* Imogen's whipping boy, indulging her every whim these days?"

He shot me a murderous glare. "Our population has exploded since President Parker took office. More and more vampires are losing their jobs, their homes. Many are being imprisoned on false charges."

"Tell me about it," I muttered.

He gave me an alert glance. "You said you were in trouble. What happened?"

"I'll explain it all to your queen when we see her. No point in telling the story twice."

He looked annoyed but didn't ask twice. "Most of all, Imogen has changed," he said. "She's less patient than she used to be."

I nearly did a spit take. "*Less* patient? Is that even possible?"

"You'll see. She's no longer content to sit idly by in the safety of our stronghold while out in the world, the injustices against our species multiply."

"I can hardly believe I'm saying this, but I sort of agree with her. Maybe peace at any cost *isn't* the answer."

In my case, the cost had almost been my life. How many other peaceful vampires, like Nathaniel Bradford and poor little Margaret and all the vampires who worked at the VHC, had lost their lives simply because they were the "wrong" species?

Like me and Kelly and Heather—and Sadie—they'd followed the rules, tried to do the right thing.

"But I'm not sure what the answer *is*. What's Imogen planning to do?"

"I'm not at liberty to talk about it. She'll share that with you if she chooses to," Reece said. "You remember your court etiquette, don't you?"

"Of course. Bow, address her as 'my queen,' don't piss her off and get myself beheaded. It hasn't been *that* long since I was here."

"You don't think so?" he said with a faint smile. "Feels like an eternity to me."

32

A WISE CHOICE

Before I could respond to the odd remark, the doors to the throne room opened, and guards ushered us inside.

They nodded to Reece in a deferential way, and I noticed all the other queensguard did the same. Clearly he'd risen in the ranks since I'd left the Bastion. It made sense—he was Imogen's child, and she'd elevated him to her personal guard shortly after he'd joined the Bloodbound.

Was that all Reece was to her? Remembering the way she'd looked at him and touched him the last time I was in this chamber I couldn't help but wonder if she'd also made him her consort.

Her reaction to our entrance gave me no clues. In fact, she paid no notice to our approach, keeping her eyes on the pair of vampires who stood before her. They seemed to be pleading their case on some matter. A line of others waited behind them for a turn.

Imogen sat on her throne wearing a sleek black wrap dress. She was just as beautiful and unnaturally young looking as she'd been the night we'd met, the night she'd turned me. Her dark hair was up in an elegant twist, her nails and lips stained a deep scarlet.

When she eventually looked over at us, Reece bowed. "My queen."

I barely heard the words over the sound of blood rushing in my ears. Hastily, I performed an awkward bow of my own.

Imogen rose from the throne and swept her arm toward the line of supplicants in a gesture of dismissal. Her personal guard moved toward the waiting vampires, telling them it was time to leave.

Two of them flanked Imogen as she descended the steps in front of the throne and walked toward me and Reece.

Actually, "walked" wasn't quite the right word. "Sashayed," would have been more accurate.

She wore a look of smug satisfaction. "I knew you'd be back. You have a lot of nerve showing your face here again after such betrayal, little one."

The guards on either side of her moved their respective hands to the dagger holders strapped at their waists, apparently ready to use them at a moment's notice.

Licking my lips, which had suddenly gone dry, I told her the absolute truth.

"I never meant to betray you. I was simply following my conscience."

And my heart, which was screaming for me to get as far away from Reece as possible.

"I know you didn't want me to return, but I didn't see another choice."

"Of course I wanted you to return, silly girl. You're my daughter." Her tone suggested only the dullest idiot would think otherwise. "Now... to what do I owe the pleasure of your homecoming?"

I was almost too shocked to answer. "I'm in some legal trouble. My friends and I were arrested by the human authorities. We didn't do anything wrong—they just cuffed us and took us to one of the Safety Centers."

"You mean prison camps," she corrected.

"They took our identification and money, locked our bank accounts."

"I heard about that. How unfortunate."

"You knew?"

"I know lots of things." Imogen pursed her lips, and her voice turned mocking. "Did your dear Sadie do nothing to help free you?"

Don't let her provoke you. Stay calm. Keep your head. Literally.

"I'm sure she would have if she'd known where we were or what had happened to us. When we escaped, I was unable to reach her. There was an attack on the Vampire-Human Coalition headquarters. It's been destroyed."

"I heard about that too. Pity."

In spite of Imogen's sympathetic words, there was no trace of compassion or concern in her demeanor. Her lack of shock certainly led weight to the possibility that she, and not human radicals, was behind the bombing.

"I don't even know if your sister is alive," I added.

"She is." Imogen's tone was matter-of-fact. "And yet you're here. What is it exactly you think *I* can do for you?"

"It isn't safe for us in the outside world anymore. The three of us are wanted—for the murder of a human. And for escaping the Safety Center. I still don't even know what the initial charges were against us that got us arrested. Anyway, our photos have been circulated nationwide. I have no idea where Sadie is now. She didn't answer her phone. We have no money, no I.D... nowhere else to turn."

Her smile held a chilling blend of pleasure and malice. "So... you've come back to my court, to beg for my protection. Perhaps you have a better understanding now of my feelings toward humans—and my disdain for my sister's approach to dealing with their species."

"In spite of what happened to me, I still believe in Sadie's teachings. I still believe in peace."

In a flash of motion, Imogen snatched the short dagger from the belt of the soldier on her right and plunged the weapon into his thigh.

The man didn't yell or react other than flinching and gasping quietly. If it had been me, I'd have dropped instantly and been rocking on the floor in pain, but he stayed upright and silent.

From the savage look on Imogen's face, I was shocked I hadn't been her target.

"How can you still be so naïve?" she roared at me. "They locked you up, hunted you—*my* daughter. It's an outrage. There can *be* no peace with them."

I was so shaken it was difficult to respond. But I had to. For Shane's sake.

"They're not all bad. There's a human who risked his life to help us get here. Shane. He took a bullet for me."

Beside me, Reece shifted slightly, and a low growl emanated from his throat.

"Yes, I'm aware of that too," Imogen said. "In fact, when I was informed you brought him *with you*—to *my* court—I almost didn't believe it. You're still capable of surprising me, little one. I'm told you actually asked our medical personnel to save his life."

She laughed out loud.

"What's funny about that? He saved my life, and Kelly's and Heather's."

"Well that's all very admirable, but you must know I can't let him leave now that he's seen our sanctuary."

"You're going to have him killed?"

She lifted one shoulder and let it fall, looking bored. "Unless you'd prefer to turn him."

The growl beside me rumbled louder. What was *with* Reece? If I could hear him, so could Imogen. Surely growling in the queen's presence wasn't in the Bloodbound rulebook.

"Of course, if you do that," Imogen said, "you must be prepared to be connected to him for eternity. You'll be his maker, and that is a very special bond."

A tremble began in my belly and worked its way outward. I spoke through quivering lips. "No. Please, Mother. You know how I feel about turning a human."

One of the reasons I'd left the Bastion was Imogen's determination to test me to see if I possessed the same "gift" she had, the ability all arch vampires had to turn a human with a single bite.

I'd skipped the Inception Ceremony on Devil's Night where the test was supposed to have happened and instead attended Sadie's speech and peaceful sit-in at the Lincoln Memorial.

It was the night I'd found my true calling and my path.

It was also the night I'd lost Reece for good when he'd chosen Imogen over me.

"I can't take someone's life. I'd rather die myself," I said.

Imogen snarled. "Very well. It will sadden me, but my primary job as queen is protecting our people against any and all threats. The needs of the many outweigh the needs of the few."

Glancing to her left, she barked an order to the Bloodbound soldier she hadn't stabbed. "Seize her. Put her in a holding cell. We'll have a public assembly in the Grand Dome tomorrow night."

Reece stepped toward the guard. "No." But he stopped himself.

Lowering the volume of his voice and dropping to a knee before Imogen, he said, "My queen, I think I may have a better solution, if you'll allow me to speak."

She gave him a fond smile, stroking the back of his downturned head and running her fingers through his shiny, dark hair. "Of course you may speak. You *are* my favorite queensguard."

As her gaze drifted back up to meet mine, there was a definite challenge in her eyes, along with a good deal of gloating. It had never been enough for her to just win—she had to rub my nose in it too.

My stomach rolled in revulsion as I pictured the two of them together. Imogen treated the Bloodbound as her own personal harem, ensuring their loyalty and obedience by having them drink her blood at their initiation.

How many times had she summoned Reece to her private chambers since I'd been gone? For all I knew it was every night. She *had* just called him her "favorite."

"You may rise," she said to him.

Straightening again, Reece kept his manner submissive. "I see this as a great opportunity, my queen. Abigail could be useful on the mission you've assigned me."

"You mean the mission *you* proposed and I approved. Yes, go on."

"She can get close to Sadie like no one else. Spare her life, and I will personally supervise her to make sure she follows your orders and doesn't get into more trouble. You can keep the human male here as... motivation."

"Wait," I said, turning to him. "What is this 'mission?'"

If it was another assassination attempt on Sadie, I'd have no part in it. I really *would* rather die than bring any harm to her.

Reece had clearly been proposing Imogen hold Shane hostage to ensure my cooperation, but if it came to a choice between saving Shane's life or Sadie's, there *was* no choice. The future of the world rested on her capable shoulders.

Imogen answered for him. "Reece has suggested, quite wisely, that there is strength in numbers. We are strong here at the Bastion, but there aren't enough of us to wage war on the entirety of the human race. We need to bring vampire-kind together under united leadership. Even before the attack on the VHC, Reece volunteered to go to my sister and convince her of this fact."

Her sharp gaze bounced between the two of us.

"He's right. Sadie's fondness for you will make her more receptive to meeting with him and listening to what he has to say. I'll allow it."

Hope sparked to life inside me. If I was allowed to meet with Sadie, there was a chance all of this could work out. Having the two vampire factions join forces was a fantastic idea.

Of course in my version of things, the newly united vampires would decide to follow Sadie's leadership instead of Imogen's.

It could happen. They just needed to be given a chance to meet her, to hear her speak.

Reece's tense posture relaxed slightly. "Thank you, my queen. I believe that is a wise choice."

Imogen gave him a tight smile then turned her icy gaze on me. "Let's hope Abigail is wise in *her* choices. Remember, little one, as you go out into the world again tomorrow and reunite with your beloved 'leader,' that I have your friend, Shane."

"Please don't hurt him," I whispered, getting choked up. "He doesn't deserve it."

"His fate is entirely in your hands. If you return with good news, if you convince Sadie to instruct her followers to join the vampire resistance, I will free him. You have my word. However... if you should try to escape or decide to stay with Sadie and never return, well then, we'll make good use of your human boyfriend's blood. In addition, your friends Kelly and Heather will be expelled."

She punctuated her threats with a friendly smile. "Travel safely, children."

33

CHARITY CALL

The following night, I went to the medical clinic to check on Shane and say goodbye.

I wasn't sure how to tell him he was a human bargaining chip.

Maybe I wouldn't. He had enough to worry about just trying to recover from a gunshot wound.

Reece accompanied me. As I was no longer an official citizen of the Bastion, he'd been assigned to watch my every move. He'd even slept outside the door of my room instead of going to the Bloodbound barracks. Imogen was nothing if not careful.

I had to walk quickly to keep up with his rapid pace. "What's the hurry?"

"I want to get this over with and get on the road. There's no time for this little charity call of yours... unless there's more to your relationship with this human than charity and friendship?"

He slid a quick glance at me.

Was he jealous? If so, it made no sense. He was the one

who'd chosen to be bound to Imogen, essentially forcing me to leave him behind.

"Shane's a very good person," I said. "And he's been a good friend. I care about him, and I have to make sure he's okay before I leave. Are you sure he'll be safe here while I'm gone?"

"I'm sure," Reece said, seeming not too thrilled about that fact. "I gave the order personally."

We walked a few moments in silence before he gestured toward the pendant I still wore around my neck. "I'll replace that for you. It's broken."

My hand automatically went to it, clasping it protectively. "No, thank you. I'll hang onto it. I... like the safety of having a weapon nearby if I need it."

What I didn't say was how much comfort having the small sample of his blood nearby had given me while we were apart and how much it had meant to me that he'd given me anything at all.

It was pointless to talk of such things and would only make me seem more pathetic than I actually was. In fact, I changed the subject.

"So, Imogen said you were already planning to go and see Sadie in Los Angeles?"

He gave a terse nod and answered without meeting my gaze. "I thought it would be smart. We'll still be outnumbered even if all the vampires join together, but we'd be a formidable minority. And Sadie would make a good emissary between the human authorities and Imogen, who of course will lead the resistance."

"Why you?"

"What do you mean?"

"Why would *you* be the one to travel to Los Angeles?"

Where I was living. Where we might have run into each other at the VHC.

His shoulders lifted and fell in a casual shrug. "Why not me? It was my idea to join forces."

Ah. So it had nothing to do with the fact I was in California. At least not as far as he was willing to admit.

"Why do you think Sadie will listen to you? I'm not sure you understand how committed she is to peace."

"I'm not sure *you* understand how close she came to dying in an explosion," he countered. "Maybe she wouldn't have listened to me before, but I'll bet she's a whole lot more interested in the concept of a vampire resistance movement now."

"Did Imogen have something to do with the attack? Please tell me it wasn't the Bloodbound who did it and pinned the blame on humans."

"Who can say who's responsible? It doesn't really matter. If it ends up being the catalyst to unite the vampire population of this country, then it was a good thing."

My jaw dropped open. "People died in that explosion, Reece. Good people. You really *have* changed, haven't you?"

I couldn't help adding, "I noticed you and Imogen are quite close."

As queen, Imogen had anytime-access to all the members of the Bloodbound, but she seemed to prefer Reece over all the others. And who could blame her? If I were queen, he'd be my "favorite," too.

He rolled his eyes. "She's my maker. She's yours, too, and you'd do well to remember it. It's the only reason you're still alive. Anyone else who'd gone and consorted with the enemy would have found themselves headless."

"Yes, I guess I should be grateful Imogen is so *merciful*." My words were laced with sarcasm, but then I got serious.

In spite of Reece's gruff attitude, he'd kept me from harm last night with his suggestion of compromise. Perhaps deep down inside somewhere he still cared for me? At least enough to not want me dead.

"Thank you for what you did, by the way, stepping in with Imogen like that."

For a moment our gazes connected and held, the tension strung between us in a taut, invisible wire. Then he gave a slight *no big deal* shrug.

"I was just being honest. I *do* think you'll be of use. Besides, like I said, I don't believe Imogen really wanted to kill you. She still has high hopes for your future."

I snorted. "Well, she can hope all she wants but there's no way I'll ever be her mini-me—now or thousands of years from now."

WHEN WE ARRIVED at the clinic, Reece insisted on going into the medical holding room with me.

"I won't say a word," he promised when I tried to protest. We entered the room together, and he went to stand against the back wall as I tiptoed to Shane's bedside.

Shane was sleeping. He looked much better, cleaned up, and his color was good. He'd been deathly pale the last time I'd seen him.

Stroking his bare arm softly, I said, "Shane? Can you hear me?"

His eyes blinked open. He looked at the ceiling and then around the room. When his gaze landed on me, he smiled.

"Abigail. Hi. Are you okay?"

"Am I okay? I came to see how *you're* doing. How do you feel? Are you in pain?"

His brows quirked as he thought about it a moment. "No, actually. They must have some good drugs at this hospital. Where are we?"

Darting a glance at Reece's glowering face, I kept my answer vague. "We're at the place I mentioned. I'm so sorry you were wounded. I was hoping you'd be on a plane or maybe even home by now."

Looking more alert, Shane pushed up to his elbows. "We're in the vampire place? It looks like a hospital room... without windows."

"It's a medical clinic. They treated you last night," I explained. "They're going to make sure you heal properly and keep you safe until I get back."

His brows pulled together. "Where are you going?"

"I have to leave for a while. I'll be back soon, I promise."

Now Shane sat up fully, placing a hand on his abdomen and patting it in apparent amazement. "It doesn't hurt at all."

He pulled up his t-shirt, exposing his mid-section. "I'm completely healed. It looks like I wasn't even shot. How is this possible?"

"They injected you with vampire blood. It heals people —that's a secret by the way."

In fact, it had been so secret, even I hadn't known about it until Dr. Coppa told me. Kannon, the big liar, had told me just the opposite in the van so I wouldn't further weaken myself by giving Shane my own blood. Besides, it had to be injected to work for humans—drinking it wasn't helpful to them.

"Don't tell anyone, okay?" I said. "We'll be even more endangered than we already are."

Shane reached out and took my hand. "I'd never do anything to endanger you. You know that."

Behind him, Reece made an irritated snorting sound.

I withdrew my hand from Shane's. "I know. And I'll make sure you stay safe, too. That's why I have to leave. I have to go and talk to Sadie."

Swinging his legs around, Shane slid from the bed and stood.

"Great. I'll go with you. When do we leave?"

34

——————

NO KOOL-AID FOR ME

"**Y**ou can't." ·

Placing a hand on Shane's chest, I urged him to sit back on the bed. "And you shouldn't get up yet. Wait for Dr. Coppa to clear you. You can trust him, by the way. He won't hurt you. He'll keep an eye on you until I return."

I could see in Shane's eyes the realization was hitting him. He craned his neck around and saw Reece, no doubt mistaking him for a security guard.

"They won't *let* me go with you, will they? Am I..." His question turned into a statement. "I'm a prisoner."

I nodded. "I'm sorry. I didn't want this to happen. I guess I didn't think it through very well when I brought you here, but you were dying and there wasn't much time. I didn't know what else to do."

"You could have turned me," he said.

I was shaking my head no, but he went on, grabbing both my hands now. "You still could. Then I could come with you. I could help you if you turn me."

"No."

"Why not? Think about it. It would be *safer* for me. I'd be

193

like you—and my parents. And they'd have no reason to keep me prisoner here. I'd be free."

This time I didn't drop his hands but squeezed them. "Shane... if I turn you... you'll *never* be free. You don't know what it's like. You would regret your decision."

"Not if I got to stay with you," he argued. "And it would solve that whole I-can't-date-a-human-guy problem."

Another disgusted snort came from Reece's side of the room.

Shane twisted to look back at him. "You wanna mind your own business buddy? I realize you hate humans, but this has nothing to do with you. Just do your job."

Reece was in Shane's face in an instant. He glared down at the shorter guy. "My *job*—is keeping the princess safe. I won't let anything get in the way of that—certainly not her *pity* for a weak human."

"Princess?" Shane gave me a quizzical look.

I cringed. "My mother is the ruler here, she's sort of... a queen."

He blinked. "Oh. Wow. Well, I guess that explains your reaction when I kissed you the first time."

Now Reece didn't snort in disgust but growled a low rumble that vibrated through me and must have raised every hair on Shane's body.

What was *up* with him? No, Shane shouldn't have told him to shut up. That would've angered any red-blooded man, human or otherwise. But Reece was being extra-aggressive toward my friend.

I put my hand on his arm. "Please. Could you give me a minute to say goodbye? Then we can go."

He maintained his stare-off with Shane for another long moment then whirled away, going to stand by the door with his hand gripping the handle so hard I worried it would break off and trap us all in this room together.

That wouldn't end well.

Shane watched him walk away. "You're traveling with *him*? I don't like it."

I smirked. "Join the club. He's leading the mission, and I'm going along to assist. Believe me, you don't want to go on this trip, and you *don't* want to turn. You shouldn't get any more involved with this world than you already are. I promised to let you return to your life, and I'll do whatever I have to do to keep that promise."

Shane reached out and cupped my face in his hands. "You're *part* of my life now. A big part. I don't want to lose you."

And then he pulled me toward him and placed a soft kiss on my lips. I gasped and drew back, staring at him in shock.

"Why did you do that?"

He lifted a sardonic brow. "You really have to ask?"

"You said you were content with being just friends."

"'Content' is a strong word for it," he said. "'Resigned' is more like it. Go do what you have to do. And when you come back, Abigail, I think we should give it a shot."

From the doorway, Reece barked, "Time's up. We need to go."

I looked from his angry violet eyes to Shane's sincere brown ones. "Goodbye—for now. I *will* come back and free you."

"I'd rather you came back and kept me." He smiled. "Be safe. I'll be waiting."

AFTER WALKING in silence for several minutes through the caverns, Reece finally spoke. His tone was dark. And accusatory.

"So you *are* interested in him."

I wasn't. But I *was* interested in Reece's reaction to Shane kissing me. He was not acting like someone who didn't care.

"What does it matter to you?" I challenged. "You knew when you joined the Bloodbound, I'd find someone else eventually. Or did you think I'd stay alone forever, pining away for you?"

If he *had* assumed that, he would have been right, but I wasn't going to tell him that.

He shot me a sullen look. "No. But *that* guy? Really? A human?"

"I work for the Vampire-Human Coalition," I said as if that explained everything. "We're all about vampires and humans getting along."

With another harumphing noise, he turned away. "There *is* no Vampire-Human Coalition anymore."

Noticing our surroundings, I realized we were heading for the throne room again. "I thought you were in a hurry to leave."

"I am. But Imogen wants to speak with you first."

"What about?" Panic raised the timbre of my voice and made my knees nearly too stiff to walk. I'd thought I was done with Imogen—at least for a while.

"I'm not sure. In spite of your accusation that we're 'close,' she rarely explains herself to me," Reece drawled.

No, she's too busy jumping your bones.

The thought of the two of them together filled my soul with bitterness. I couldn't keep it from spilling over into my voice.

"So how many Bloodbound is your *queen* sending along to protect her 'favorite soldier?'"

He shot me a look of bitter annoyance. "None."

Suddenly there seemed to be no air in the cavern. The pulse point in the side of my neck started tapping.

"It's just the two of us?" I wheezed.

"Yep. A happy little couple on a cross-country vacation."

His tone oozed sarcasm. We weren't a couple anymore, and we were far from happy.

But I was struck by the fact that destiny had brought us together again. At the beginning of this week, I had been on the opposite side of the country with no thought of ever coming back to this place—or to him. And now here we were together, preparing to embark on a journey together.

Just the two of us.

Oh, this is not *good.*

"I thought you said Imogen considered this mission a top priority."

"She does," Reece said. "And that's why we have to avoid attracting too much human attention. Traveling with a group of Bloodbound wouldn't exactly be subtle."

"Oh." That much was true. All the vampire soldiers were like Reece—jacked and extremely tall.

If the females here couldn't stop staring, then human women would gawk non-stop. And human men would notice *that* if nothing else.

"Reece... I've been wondering... why *are* you all so... well, you know?"

He looked over at me and actually grinned a little. "No. So... what?"

"You know what I'm asking. Why are you all so big? Why do you look so... good?"

The grin widened. "I told you, we have a special diet."

"Right. You said your blood bags come from a special supply. What's so special about it?"

"It's mixed with Imogen's blood. Which reminds me." He pulled a small vial from his pocket, handing it to me. "Drink up."

Holding it up to the light, I studied it. The vial was filled with blood.

"Wait... is this Imogen's? I don't want it. This is what keeps all of you loyal to her no matter what. No Kool-Aid for me, thank you."

I tried to give it back to him, but he refused to take it. "Queen's orders. She'll know if you haven't taken it."

"Oh. *That's* why she wants to see me. She should know she doesn't have to force me to go along with the plan. She's holding Shane hostage. I'm not going to let any harm come to him."

"Of course you wouldn't. He's too 'important,'" Reece said, mocking the word I'd used earlier when speaking with the doctor. "But I don't think that's it. It probably has more to do with your appearance."

"My appearance?"

I looked down at myself, at the inconspicuous dark jeans and boots and the black leather jacket I wore. "What's wrong with how I look?"

"Nothing. You look... fine. It's just we're not going to get very far if you're recognized as a fugitive."

"So, I'll wear a disguise. That's what I did to get out of San Francisco."

"You won't need a disguise if you'll just do as you're told and drink that."

Inspecting the vial again, I asked, "Imogen's blood will change my appearance?"

"Not completely. But enough to fool the humans."

Seeing my reluctance, he added, "Look, it's your choice, but if you don't drink it, you can't come with me. And if you don't come with me and at least try to help me get through to Sadie, Imogen will have no reason to keep your little human sweetie-pie alive. Old Shane's gonna find himself the main course at dinner tonight because you're squeamish about drinking a little royal blood."

"Fine." I yanked the cap from the vial and downed its contents. "How long does the magic pretty-potion take?"

"You're already—" Reece stopped himself and started again. "It'll take a few hours to alter your appearance significantly. And another dose or two to enable you to mesmerize humans."

35

A LOVELY TRIP

"What did you say?"

I wasn't sure which of his statements was more shocking—the one where he'd (almost) complimented me or the one where he'd hinted at vampires having supernatural mind control powers.

"Mesmerize. Humans," he said, choosing to address only the latter of the two.

"We can't do that."

"Some of us can. The Bloodbound can. Imogen calls it 'the pull.' I call it useful. Especially now that cars are checked at every state border. And we'll be crossing quite a few of them in the next few days."

"Are we going back to California? Do you know where Sadie is?"

"I don't know exactly. But Imogen has a sense of where to find her. She's not in California. She's in Canada. Makes sense—they're much more vampire-friendly there these days than the U.S. is."

Reaching the throne room doors, Reece stopped, clearly intending to wait outside.

"She wants to see you alone. She specifically said she didn't want me there."

"Oh."

Had Imogen changed her mind about me and decided to go ahead and end my annoying, disappointing existence? Maybe she worried Reece would try to intervene and prevent the execution.

The fear in my eyes must have been obvious because his tone softened considerably. "It'll be okay. I'll be right here waiting."

I took a deep breath and let it out slowly before nodding and going inside. The throne room was deserted except for Imogen. If there was to be an execution, she intended to do it herself.

As I got close, she smiled that beautiful, cold smile of hers. "How is your friend, Shane, doing tonight? Much improved, I hope?"

"Yes. He's better," I answered through lips stiff with dread.

"That's good news. It would be a shame for an innocent human to lose his life over you."

I decided to just be blunt with her. "Look, you don't need the thinly veiled threats or even direct ones. I know you'll kill Shane if I don't cooperate."

"Oh, that's a given. What I want you to understand is, he's not the *only* one who'll pay the price if you fail. I'll dispose of everyone you care about—including the one you care for most."

The breath evaporated from my lungs. "Reece. You wouldn't."

"Don't doubt it for a moment."

"But... he's your child. You said you hadn't created a child in over a hundred years before turning the two of us."

"That's true," Imogen said, drawing out the last word.

She lifted a hand and tapped her lips with one slender, manicured fingertip. "Have I ever told you what happened to the children I created in the past? No? It's not exactly bedtime story material, I'm afraid. Might cause nightmares. Let it suffice to say you don't want to disappoint me."

"I'll speak to Sadie," I vowed. "And I'll make sure she gives Reece an audience and considers your offer. All I can do is my best, and I promise you I will."

"I'm glad to hear it. There's one more thing before you go..."

She rose and came to stand directly in front of me. "Do not forget the promise *Reece* has made—to me. He's made an eternal commitment to serve me... and me only. He's useless to me if he's not loyal. In every way."

"What are you saying?"

"I'm not blind. He has a certain... weakness for you."

I blinked hard, biting the inside of my cheek to suppress a warm, sweet rush of foolish joy. Her words shouldn't make me feel that way, and I *really* shouldn't let her see the inappropriate involuntary reaction.

"You're wrong. He hasn't shown the least bit of interest in me since I've been back."

"Be that as it may, I'm advising you—strongly—not to tempt him to violate any of the Bloodbound rules."

Imogen gave me a coy smile and raised one perfectly arched brow. "If any vows *are* broken, Reece is the one who'll pay the price—with his life. And I'll make sure *you* live forever so you can fully appreciate his loss."

Then she turned and walked slowly back to her throne where she sat primly with her hands in her lap.

"You are dismissed. Have a lovely trip."

EPILOGUE

When I emerged from the throne room, Reece was there waiting as promised.

And he was smiling.

Not a fake one this time—the real thing.

It made him even more devastatingly handsome than ever, but it also worried me a little. What on earth was there to be so happy about? We were embarking on a do-or-die mission, and our relationship wasn't exactly a smooth one.

"Did someone just tell you a great joke or something?" I asked as we fell into step together, headed for the cavern's exit.

Still smiling, he shook his head. "No. I just saw Kannon. We had a good talk."

"About?"

"Nothing much. Guy stuff."

"But it made you happy?"

The grin widened even further. "Yes. It. Did."

"Ooookay then."

Clearly Reece wasn't going to tell me about their conversation. At least he was pleasant for a change instead of being the surly ogre he'd been since my return to the Bastion.

Glancing over at me, he said, "Look, I figured some things out when we were talking, okay? Come on, Abbi. I'd think you'd be happy to bid farewell to the cranky SOB you found when you got here."

Not only was he still smiling, but he *sounded* like the old Reece—*my* Reece—the guy I'd met that night under the Crimson Moon. The guy he'd been before taking the Blood-bound vows.

"I am glad," I said cautiously. "I mean, it would have been a long drive to Canada otherwise."

"Exactly. As long as we're traveling together, we might as well have a good time, right?"

I hesitated, but finally said, "Right."

In spite of our agreement, my senses were on high alert. Maybe I was just nervous. Convincing Sadie to align with Imogen and agree to joint leadership of the vampire people promised to be challenging.

Traveling with Reece—alone—possibly for weeks —*without* giving into my attraction to him would be even more difficult.

Maybe impossible.

Especially if he was going to be charming like this.

But I couldn't fail either mission. Lives, including Shane's and Reece's, hung in the balance.

My mother—my real one—used to say, "You never know how strong you are until being strong is the only choice you have."

Well, I was about to find out once and for all the measure of my own strength.

I could only pray it would be enough.

THANK you for reading **Crimson Storm**, Book 2 of the Crimson Accord series. If you enjoyed it, would you consider writing a quick review? There's no wrong or right way to write a review—a few words is all it takes, and reviews are very important. They help authors more than you know and help other readers find great books. Thank you!

Thirsty for more Crimson? Book 3, **Crimson Bond**, is available now in ebook and print and soon to come in audio! Turn the page for a look at the cover and a sneak peek at the story.

I never thought I'd see her again. Never dared to hope. But against all odds, Abigail's back.

Unfortunately she's as sweet as ever and even more beautiful.

And I'm in serious trouble.

I've learned to hate Abbi in the time she's been away, but the blazing attraction between us is still there. And now, having her close enough to touch—close enough to taste—I'm in a literal battle for my life.

Because my Bloodbound oath still holds, and the punishment for breaking it is still death.

The last thing I want is "alone time" with her, but that's exactly what I get when the queen sends me on a mission, and the only way to keep Abbi alive is to take her with me.

In this third book of the Crimson Accord series, the rift between humans and vampires widens, the menace of the Crimson Court intensifies, and the temptation for Reece and Abigail grows to a fever pitch.

Will they give in to it? Or will the dangerous secrets that stand between them destroy their chance of love and any hope of living in peace? Grab your copy of Crimson Bond today and find out!

AFTERWORD

Thank you so much for reading Crimson Storm, book two of my new Crimson Accord series. I hope you enjoyed it! If you did, I'd be so grateful if you'd leave a review on the retailer where you purchased it and if your fingers aren't too tired, on Goodreads as well. It's not hard to do—just a few words about what you thought of the book is perfectly fine. Reviews are so important for authors and help other readers find great books.

The series continues with book three, **Crimson Bond**, available now on all ebook retailers and in paperback.

Members of my VIP mailing list receive notifications whenever I have a new book release or special sale—plus a free book! I'd love to have you join. Here's where to do that: https://bit.ly/APsVIPs

If you love a good fantasy escape, be sure to also check out my completed Hidden Saga series. Book 1, Hidden Deep, has sold more than than 400,000 copies and has more than 2500 5-star reviews, and good news—the ebook is FREE to download for a limited time!

Turn the page to check out the series...

THE COMPLETE CRIMSON ACCORD SERIES

Reading order:

Crimson Born

Crimson Storm

Crimson Bond

Crimson Crown

ALSO BY AMY PATRICK

THE HIDDEN SAGA- COMPLETE AND READY TO BINGE!

Hidden Deep

Hidden Heart

Hidden Hope

The Sway (FREE when you join my list!)

Hidden Darkness (Dark Court, 1)

Hidden Danger (Dark Court, 2)

Hidden Desire (Dark Court, 3)

Hidden Game (Ancient Court, 1)

Hidden Magic (Ancient Court, 2)

Hidden Hero (Ancient Court, 3)

Hidden Heir

The Hidden Saga is in audiobook! Books 1-6 are available in audio now. Books 7-9, the Ancient Court subset containing Hidden Game, Hidden Magic, and Hidden Hero, will release in audio soon. You can also listen to books 1 and 2 of the Crimson Accord series in audio! The rest of the series is coming soon in audiobook format.

ABOUT THE AUTHOR

Amy Patrick writes "unique" and "engrossing" (Examiner. com) romantic fiction and young adult fantasy/paranormal books that make you want to "read straight through the night into the breaking hours of dawn." (Bitten By Books)

Her hugely popular Hidden Saga is now joined by her new Crimson Accord series, a young adult vampire romance saga.

Follow Amy on Bookbub to receive notices about her new releases and sales, and join her VIP mailing list at https://bit.ly/APsVIPs for all the latest book news, insider info, and fun freebies.

Amy is a multi-award-winning author and two-time RWA Golden Heart finalist and lives in Rhode Island where she enjoys writing at the beach year round. She's been a professional singer, voiceover artist, and TV news anchor, and currently writes fiction full time as well as narrating audiobooks.

For more, visit her website—http://www.amypatrick-books.com/

Oxford South Press/December 2020

Editing by Judy Roth

Cover by Emily Cover Design